FAR AFIELD

Far Afield

A Novel

SCOTT BROWN

 RED HEN PRESS | *Los Angeles, CA*

Far Afield
Copyright © 2009 by Scott Brown

Book layout by Sydney Nichols

Library of Congress Cataloging-in-Publication Data

Brown, Scott Shibuya.
  Far afield / Scott Brown. — 1st ed.
    p. cm.
  ISBN 978-1-59709-424-5
  1. Journalists—Fiction. 2. Asian Americans—Fiction. 3. South
Pacific Ocean—Fiction. 4. Oceania—Fiction. I. Title.
  PS3602.R72286F37 2009
  813'.6—dc22

                              2009031768

The Annenberg Foundation, the James Irvine Foundation, the Los Angeles County Arts Commission, and the National Endowment for the Arts partially support Red Hen Press.

First Edition

Published by Red Hen Press
Los Angeles, CA
www.redhen.org

For this book, many thanks to Chris Abani,
my agent Sara Crowe, Kate Gale, and Cristina Garcia.
And, of course, to my parents, Al and Akiko.

For my daughter, Pilar

Part One

I

I DIDN'T PLAN to go to Momo-Jima, but then no one really plans to go to Momo-Jima. The natives tell you that soon after you put down at Dunbar-dori Airport and take the short moko-moko ride to the offhand triangle of worn-out trinket shops and sad, dirty hotels in Ueda Town Center (a six-minute ride, tops). Indeed, what interests them most is how you've happened to come to their country—or been waylaid, as some of them will outright admit—and often after hearing your story they will offer a few in return from some of the others who've preceded you. Then a tremendously over-priced welcoming drink is prepared and waiting for you in your hotel room, and from there the real business of rapacity begins. In my case, I went for several reasons, none of which were outstand-ing by themselves to warrant my trip. But more about that, and my tangle of motivations, later. If it was peculiarity that led me here, it was a greater peculiarity that kept me. And if it has taken me longer to figure out the contours of the situation I was escaping, as well as the one I entered into, perhaps it is because the difficulty of fleeing our circumstances also increases with age.

At any rate, I'd scheduled myself for twelve days on Momo-Jima, my usual yearly vacation. This time, I was hoping to use my hiatus to think somewhat deeply about a book I was writing on ancient sports (in my working life, I am a freelance journalist), though I suspect what I really was after was an escape from the pressure its existence was exerting on me at home. Still, in a good faith effort

I'd brought a small trunk of materials on the history of athletics, along with my laptop and a dozen pencils, multicolored pens and legal pads. I envisioned myself absorbing their contents at poolside, sustained by a steady stream of drinks, or perhaps prostrate on one of the beaches with the ocean sounds nudging me on. They had a spectacular one here, according to my guidebook—a two-mile-long stretch of sand that had been dyed pink some years back in a bid to attract tourists. Though it hadn't succeeded (given that the color had an adverse affect on the island's native gulls, many of which began attacking the beachgoers who ventured onto the sand), the shore still retained a patina that had faded from its original color into a warmer, more beckoning hue. Or, again, so I'd read in my guidebook.

So barely an hour after my jetliner had set down on the wide concrete slab that functioned as the national airport, I was forging manfully ahead onto the painted sands with several volumes of sports arcana and two bottles of the local beer in hand. Doing so, I felt the thrill that accompanies the first foray of any vacation, be it in a congested European metropolis or on an island hideaway. "This is what you came for," the moment implies and before any disillusionment or restlessness has set in, it is easy to believe that you are about to get what you are seeking.

Even still, I had to acknowledge that it was rather a dismal Momo-Jiman plain that now stretched out in front of me. Years of gull shit had stained the now salmon-hued sands with voluminous patches of white and green, around which people had carefully picked their way and settled their oversized blankets. And though the temperature was warm, the sky was leaden gray, with only a small amount of sun penetrating the thick clouds that threatened a tropical rain. Yet I also saw there was a smattering of beachgoers gamely out trying to make a day of it. From the old and splintering boardwalk above, I watched them turning themselves over with regularity on the sands as if to evenly absorb as much as they could of the paltry sunlight. There is nothing like the determination of vacationers out to get full value on their time off.

With my bulky knapsack filled with my books, papers, and beer, I joined them, eager to begin my vacation after a year without break, a five-thousand-mile trek and some ten hours of flight. Despite the overcast, the ground was warm as I unfolded my blanket on a clean, unsmeared patch of sand and lay down flat against the earth. Only a few minutes earlier, I had been travelling some ten thousand feet above this very spot. I briefly wondered what I would see if I viewed myself sprawled lazily on this pink beach, one abstracted figure lying amidst so many others. Probably only another spoiled tourist concerned with that day's exchange rates, the number of hours to lunch, and perhaps arranging an evening rendezvous. Opening my pack, I then pulled out a thick book on Aztec history (sport having played a large, if bloody, role in the smooth running of that civilization) and a bottle of beer and propped myself up to read. A moment later, I thought better of it, put the book down, turned myself over and fell asleep, drowsy and content at my safe arrival.

After several minutes, however, I was awakened by a grinning and oversized man; standing over me, his girth had suddenly and completely blocked out the sun, which had now appeared in full force. Startled, I jerked myself up into a sitting position. Though I had passed out for only a brief time, my arms and legs felt heavy, as if I'd been under a narcotized sleep, and it took an effort to move them.

"Good afternoon," said the man in a hollow baritone.

I reached for my glasses—the lenses now misted with a layer of dried salt—put them on and saw in front of me a man in his late fifties with soft blue eyes, a large broken-angled nose, and thinning blond hair. On the beach, he wore heavy brown shoes and an old-fashioned tan suit. I guessed that he stood over six feet and he was hefty throughout his trunk and shoulders. His smile stayed fixed as I brushed the sand from my hands to shake his, which he was extending down to me.

"Sorry," he said in a concerned tone, seeing my disheveled manner. "I didn't mean to ambush you."

That he caught me flustered was certainly true. I am generally unaccustomed to being singled out and each time it happens, I am momentarily thrown beyond words. This reflex of mine dates back to grade school (I am now in my early forties), which was when I first noticed that I belonged to that class of people who, owing to their psychological or physical makeup, invariably go unacknowledged when it comes to recognition, both of the good and bad kind.

People like us—and there actually are fewer of us than you might think—are used to existing in relief, keeping tabs on the rest of the world, which, it seems, cannot help but bask in the light of itself. Instead, our manner is to furtively wait, an act that only confirms and solidifies our original nature, and any attempts to garner recognition only ensures us greater anonymity. Of course, it works both ways, as well. If we are unseeable, we also are unknowable and that might confer an advantage on us, if the right situation were to present itself.

Lastly, we also possess a great deal of information that would be useful if anyone bothered to ask us for it.

I stood, brushing more sand off myself. Now that I was next to him, I could see how much larger he was than me in height and breadth.

"My name's Trevor MacGower and I'd like a word with you," he said seriously.

"About what?"

"About your future."

I was about to reply, "I haven't the time," when I realized that this might seem as if I were making fun of him. So instead I managed a quizzical "Oh?" and put a look of polite interest on my face. I noticed as we stood together that he was perspiring so hard that sweat circles had appeared on the outside of his suit.

"I didn't catch your name," he inquired, continuing in the manner of a store detective.

"Ben," I said reluctantly. "Benjamin Inoue."

I winced imperceptibly. Hearing my name reminded me that I have never liked it or gotten used to it. In addition to its childish iambic meter, it always has sounded to me as if I was subliminally saying "Ben, in a way." Perhaps on occasion I have said it as such; maybe this would account for some of my at-large invisibility.

"May I call you Ben?" he asked and then leaned closer to me. "Ben, why are so many of us desperately miserable and why is unhappiness the expected order of things?"

"Sorry?"

"It is our human mystery. We are capable of creating any circumstance we wish, yet so many of us wallow in continuous displeasure. I ask you, is it our power or powerlessness that allows us to adapt to conditions that are less than acceptable?"

His voice was rapid and mellifluous and for the second time in a minute, I had no response. Simply, his words made no sense to me. I also suffered the immediate and sinking feeling (known to me from my experience as a journalist) that I was being hauled down the path of a well-intentioned lunacy. Still, I kept a look of courteous interest on my face. Politeness, whether ingrained in me by my parents or fixed on me by my profession, is a permanent and often regrettable part of my character.

"What is it you want?" I asked after a moment.

He ignored me and went on.

"Of course, everyone says life is supposed to be a sorry business," he said, "but unfortunately, this recognition is so obvious that we no longer acknowledge it. And if we can't acknowledge it, how are we to do anything about it?"

"Are you selling something? If you are, I don't have any money on me."

"Not selling a thing. Merely stating the truth for your benefit. Do you know what I read this morning in the newspaper?"

Automatically in my reporter's mode, I replied, "What?" Somehow it seemed easier to go along with his unknowable premise than to resist it. The intricacies of a person's derangement can be endless and it's pointless to try to comprehend them. Plus, despite his size, he didn't seem threatening or dangerous, only passionate over an idea, which perhaps is worse.

"There is a new service for the terminally ill," he went on. "It is now available in some of the European countries. If you haven't much longer to live, scientists can use a virtual reality machine to provide you the death you wish. They are starting a business to recruit patients. 'Peaceful Passages,' it is called."

Hearing his words, especially the word "death," gave me a sharp chill despite the overhead sun, which now was blazing away.

"You can be the captain of a battleship going down, or a king at his last banquet, or even the lover of a beautiful movie star," he said. "First you choose your scenario, then you put on the apparatus, and then you are given a lethal injection. In this small way, you leave life as you have wished. 'On your terms,' said one of the doctors."

I remained silent. The sound of the waves breaking on the shore seemed oppressively loud. Or were those my troubled thoughts now crashing together?

"But the point, the inhuman irony of it, is that you must leave life to attain what you want," he continued, his delivery more charged. "Only in death, suicide no less, can you have what you wanted in life. They called this 'progress' in the newspaper. To kill yourself to fulfill yourself! A slave to the end, then the freedom of death."

At the words "suicide" and then "kill," a change came over me and I snapped out of my reverie. For a moment, I stood staring at him as if I'd been the one rambling wildly and he was the silent and puzzled party. Then quickly gathering my books and stuffing my blanket into my knapsack, I mumbled something incoherent and hastily left the beach, stamping up the sands as fast as I could. As I hurried away, I thought I heard a strangled plea come from behind me but I didn't turn around to look.

II

FOR, YOU SEE, it was a death, among other things, that led me to this island. Not the death of a loved one, or a close relative, or even anyone I'd known. No, it was a thankfully anonymous passing, but it occurred close to me—that is, the building where I live—and I was among the first to discover the body and that is its impact on me. Several weeks later, it remains very much a live matter in one of my more guarded emotional cells, and I have been at great pains to resolve the experience.

Perhaps for all this to make sense, you should know a little about where I come from. I live in Los Angeles, the city where I was born and raised, and a place that I've left several times but to which I've always returned. It is an area with too many elements to adequately explain, yet the tendency is for people with an opinion of it to sum it up simplistically, both for the good and the bad. To avoid a similar failure of judgment, I will make no such pronouncement, and only say that the main reason I continue to live there is because it never fails to keep me interested, though not on the level of culture or politics or art as with other cities. Instead, for me, the city's most attractive feature lies in its ongoing collective failure. That is, the way its people recycle the energy they've spent pursuing their defeated dreams into celebrations of their own struggle, and thus try to retain their individuality. In this gesture (which is either tribally ancient or adamantly postmodern, depending on how you view it), there is something vulgar, yet touching and illuminating.

Failure, as I remember from the many psychology courses I took in college, is always a more powerful instructive than success.

Still, it can be a difficult place, especially for a person living by himself. In other large cities (New York comes to mind), the alone life is acceptable; that is, considering the number who do it, the residents wind up alone all together. In Los Angeles, which undergoes a daily transformation from arrivals at both ends of the economic spectrum, one is forgotten if not moving hurriedly in the pursuit of something bigger. Yet to do so requires either a profound ignorance of, or cynicism toward, the surroundings. And for natives familiar with the counterfeit history of the city (again, both in its good and bad elements), neither alternative is correct or available.

This also explains why I chose to live where I do—in an old, urban-bound residential hotel that seems oppositional to the city's nature. In Los Angeles, as far west as you can realistically go, such a choice presumably refutes the promise of the desert expanse (which, to me, instead promises infinite amounts of nothing). If there are such hotels, they must be for the old and infirm, the criminal at heart, the veteran transient or the permanently poor, so the thinking goes. Yet several of these dowager places still exist and mine, the Pimlico, is lucky in that its nearness to downtown has allowed it not to deteriorate but instead to prosper with ever-fresh cycles of Asian businessmen, high school groups from the Midwest, and earnest new screenwriters living on trust accounts or welfare. It is an anomalous thing: a bustling old hotel half-filled with residents of low and modest means and half-filled with purposeful visitors.

Moreover, it is a beautiful building: ten stories of ether white, tricked out with flaking balconies, languorous stairwells, vaulted ceilings, and lion's head moldings, the standard finishes of off-the-rack luxury. Once, I suppose, the hotel was envisioned as one of those grand statements about the triumph of the American century, but at the time it was being completed, the Depression had struck and the money for it ran out in midstream. As a result, even today there are hallways festering away unfinished and nailed shut, and the plumbing is erratic on the building's east side. Still, I have liked it ever since I moved there following my divorce eight years ago, and occasionally, I even manage the night desk for a deduction on the rent.

It is only since the suicide that I have had my second thoughts.

And please, though I keep calling it a suicide, I cannot be sure.

At any rate, it was a bizarre death, stranger than any I'd encountered in my working life, or heard of in general. It came to light early one morning towards the end of one of my overnight shifts. I was totaling up the evening receipts when one of the cleaning crew frantically called, asking that I come upstairs as quickly as possible. Though it is against the rules to leave the front desk unattended, something in her voice made me put out the "Manager Away" sign and hurry to the elevator. There was in it the notes of real human trouble and as the elevator lurched upward to the seventh floor—a nonresidence floor—I could only think that a guest had been robbed or that some other similar catastrophe had struck.

Once there, I saw that the hotel's entire maintenance staff had gathered outside a room and was talking in hushed, fearful tones. None of them had made a move to venture inside, nor did they acknowledge my presence. But thinking that whatever had occurred was a problem involving some sort of obvious and damaging malfeasance (and therefore solely my responsibility), I also hurried past them, not wanting to encourage any interference.

However, the moment I entered the room, I knew I had made a terrible mistake. Indeed, I could not have imagined a worse scenario, and had I known what lay behind the door, I certainly would not have gone in by myself. For in front of me was a dead man, and not just any dead man. This one was hung by a thin clothesline attached to one of the building's high brass fixtures and his body now slowly swung in the new currents caused by my entrance. And unfortunately, he was not naked.

Instead he was a tall man fantastically adorned: a peach-colored chemise covered his saggy and hairy chest, gray stockings went up to his thighs, paste pearls were under his throat, and black patent mules covered his large feet. A harsh slit of eyeliner was drawn over his brows and a slowly evolving pool of the evacuated fluids that fell between his shoes was collecting on the floor. The dead man also wore much dime-store jewelry: harlequin pins, rings, and attractive red earrings that dangled from his dead lobes. The tip of his mottled penis just jutted out from under the slip.

Though I had never been alone with a dead man—much less one so gaudily arrayed—my initial reaction was not one of horror but rather of great embarrassment (even recalling it now, I blush). In the face of this unequivocal display, I somehow felt that this was not just death I was viewing but instead a large and incalculable intimacy and that suddenly I was the indecent one.

As I looked around the room (also trying not to breathe too heavily of the rapidly fouling air), I then saw there was further reason for my feeling, for strewn on the floor was a good deal of open pornography. The rough stuff, too, not the kind bought at newsstands. Here were women subjected, and subjecting others, to a wide variety of fetishes that only could have been dreamed up by the most sexually industrious, or innocent. Briefly, I saw restraining devices and rubber masks, excrement on glass coffee tables, giant unnerving weapons, and many ropes and toes, all shown in graphic blowups. An English TV producer staying at the hotel once had given me a magazine like this and inside were the most lurid photos I had ever seen. More out of clinical interest, I'd kept it in my bookcase for several months but I finally threw it out after mistaking gas pains for a stroke one night and wondering who might see the magazine if I had really died.

Though it later proved to be a useless gesture, my first move was to be very careful about touching anything in the room and thus spoiling any criminal evidence. Walking in a wide arc around the body, I took a napkin from my pocket and used it to pick up the phone to dial for an ambulance. As I did so, it struck me that this pitiable call would be the last act performed on this man's behalf, the end of the thousands of things done for him since birth. I suddenly imagined babysitters and nursery schools; boxes of stuffed toys and short pants; first dances and orthodontia; then driving lessons and bank accounts, followed by the university send-off and the welcomings home; then the long entering into the adult life with its many and random needs and dependencies, including finally, the message to carry him away. Overall, I thought, there is very little in our lives for which we do not receive help. And while this last obligation was unbidden, given its place in his order of things, I somehow felt it tied me in a disconcerting way to the dead man.

Fortunately, the city's response to my queasiness was quick and efficient. Over the phone, a very young and assured-sounding dispatcher said it sounded like a bungled try at autoerotic asphyxiation. Cutting off your oxygen to boost your joy, she said. There were several calls a month to come and get the dead. Her manner was breezy and matter-of-fact and as she mentioned the condition, I suddenly recalled that I had read a newspaper article on the practice just this week. Perhaps the dead man had read and been moved by the same piece.

After that brief conversation, there was nothing to do but wait, which I decided to do in the lobby downstairs. Before I left, though, I took one last look at the body and felt a vague disappointment come over me. For after its dramatic entrance, I thought, death actually has very little to say. Nothing about the knowledge that comes with spending a lifetime with yourself, nothing about the toil of decades that breaks your heart, and nothing at all about the state of the mind when coming up on the last blind curve. Mostly, death serves simply as a reminder to the living, counseling either, "Make do, make time, struggle harder," or, depending on your place in the biological cycle, "Stop struggling, coast. It is all but over."

I studied the dead man's face but his eyes were snapped tight, his mouth was closed, and there were no clues to his final thoughts. Maybe death does have opinions, I thought, but those it keeps to itself. Reflecting on this, a sudden urge of protectiveness came over me. Taking a large towel from the bathroom, and then balancing on a shaky desk chair next to the body, I leaned in close to the dead man and threw the thin cotton fabric over his face, covering him down to his shoulders. The body swayed some in reaction, if not actual response. I then stepped off the chair, shut the blinds and left the room, opening the door as little as I could to prevent the cleaning crew outside from seeing too much of what lay inside.

III

FOR SEVERAL DAYS afterward, I muddled about in a pervasive gloom, riven by thoughts that were strange to me, and mostly unable to work. One night, still in the grip of my malaise, I struggled through an uneasy sleep, waking once, then again, then finally for good in the blackest part of the early morning. Outside my living room door, the hallway creaked with old building noises and a feeble light appeared in a crack at the bottom. Without turning on any inside lights, I went to my ninth-floor vantage and looked out.

Below me, the city was breathing quietly. The street, a clogged and suffocating boulevard by day, was empty of cars. Not one passed for more than a minute. A few lights came from closed businesses but none shone from the adjoining apartment buildings. There was not even a bus or a cop at this time of night. Where were the city dollars going? I wondered. I pulled a chair up to the window and continued to look out. Since I am not one for staying up much past midnight, the scene at this irregular hour was captivating. I must have lingered at the window for forty-five minutes looking into the murk even though there was little activity on which to focus my attention.

I realized that I would have liked to talk with someone about my recent experiences but I also knew there was no one I could engage in this. Not only could I not explain myself or my feelings, but my mostly self-contained lifestyle has left me generally free of significant company for the past several years, a fact I'd only recently begun to realize but whose potential consequences were looming larger in my consciousness. For you had to watch it while living alone. Isolation freed you from the gauntlet of daily scrutiny but it could invest you with irregular personal habits. Like peeing in the shower (I didn't) or cutting up shopping bags to use as coffee filters (I sometimes did). Accumulate too many odd behaviors and your solitude would be ensured, something doubly true if you began to have your groceries delivered or attached yourself to pets. Every once in a while, such a person died and the newspapers would make much of what was found inside their homes.

It was then that I suddenly thought of calling my ex-wife, Stella, for though we are divorced, we have remained on friendly, if distant terms. And though we separated over an infidelity (hers, with a meagerly talented sculptor), the fact that she eventually married the man made it easier for me to absorb the split and undertake a partial friendship. At any rate, I've held no permanent grudge. In retrospect, I've wondered how great my commitment was to her, as well, and whether this played a part in her eventual leaving.

After a few more moments, I reached for the phone and dialed. She now lived in New Jersey with the sculptor, Rodni, and ran a small photography studio. Though it would be early morning there, they both were early risers, getting up everyday to greet the dawn or some such spiritual nonsense. Likewise, my voice would not come as a complete surprise. Though we rarely spoke, occasionally we exchanged letters and always she sent me holiday cards—for Christmas, Rosh Hashanah, Kwanzaa, the Muslim holy days, the Chinese New Year, etc. One year she mailed a greeting for the summer solstice. Opening it, I could not help but smile at how seriously she took matters of the earth.

"Hello?"

She picked up immediately and her voice sounded older than I remembered. Did mine sound the same?

"Stella, it's Ben."

"How nice, Ben. I was just thinking about you. Listen, what was the name of the place where we used to get the jerk chicken? It could make your tongue bleed."

"Bistamante's."

"Bistamante's, that's right. I knew you'd know."

She yelled the name of the restaurant over her shoulder, then came back to me.

"So. So how are you?"

"Not so good."

"You sound nervous."

I then told her about the dead man. Though it was a long tale I left out no details and elaborated more than I usually do (normally, I am the most direct of storytellers). Oddly, while relating the events, I found I became partially relieved; it was if I was bringing another person into what had felt like a conspiracy against my deeper view of reality.

"Well that's very strange, a man like that," she said when I finished. "But what does that have to do with living by yourself? Are you saying this is something you'd like to do? If you are, I would be careful. Get a book on it or something."

"No, no, I just meant . . ."

I closed my eyes. Have indulgence, I told myself. At least she was listening. In the past, whenever I used to try to interest her in the spectral matters she would say, "I'm sick of these questions, I want something to eat." Now thanks to Rodni she had built up a taste for such blather.

Hearing her, too, made me think of the house where my voice was now entering. I could well picture it. Lots of artistic clutter and overpriced, worthless doodads. Cat hair on the sofa and paint on the wooden furniture. Sticky floors in the kitchen. Stella was unnaturally sloppy, unaware of the distinction between dirt and disorder. I recalled thinking when we were married that her mess created another living entity. Once, while rummaging through her books, I found that she had used a wrapped piece of cheese as a bookmark. The pages had stained pale yellow where the coloring of the cheese had seeped, while inside the cellophane was crumbled black dusty mold. Had this occurred before we were married, I would have found it almost endearing.

"It just struck me as cruel that this man should die by himself like this," I said. "And then with everyone getting to see him."

"People die by themselves every day. We can't take anyone with us. And if he didn't want people to look, he shouldn't have dressed up. What a getup! Did you say he had pearls on, too?"

"But the end, when he was struggling with the clothesline. It's awful to think that there was no one there."

"It sounded like he wanted to be alone."

"Nobody wants to die alone."

"That's not true. What about the Eskimos on the ice floes? They don't load up the family to come watch. Some things are private."

Stella paused.

"I think it's kind of comforting, if you ask me. At least he died doing what he wanted."

"That's not what I mean. Doesn't memory count for anything? Some people think that memories are living things, that they take up real space and keep us entertained whenever we call on them. Think of the memories this man left behind. How can he rest leaving an impression like that in the world?"

My frustration was showing. She was silent. I relented a bit.

"I'm asking you because you know me. Better than anyone." (I winced at this.) "Is what I'm telling you crazy?"

"Oh, Ben, don't ask me that. I don't know you anymore to answer."

I felt my insides slip. It was a frailty leveled but it was true. Marriages ran on the balance of information—who had it, who was keeping it. They fell apart when people stopped believing the same information or miscalculated the amount they could share and the amount they could keep to themselves. Stella was right. She had no way of knowing me, anymore.

"Say you didn't know me, then. What would you think?"

Stella sighed, a queenly exhale of breath. She put her hand over the phone and began speaking, presumably to Rodni. After a lengthy exchange, she returned..

"Rodni has something to tell you. I'm not sure if it's an Arabic saying or whether he just likes saying it that way. But I'll put him on. He'll help you."

Before I could object, Rodni's sonorous voice was traveling the interstate phone lines, his full lips audibly pressed to the receiver. His was an overly ripe mind, full of charged opinions and repudiations, which he dispensed with an angry sense of beneficence. He probably licked the phone when he talked, too, I thought.

"Ben, how are you? I'll keep it short. Are you listening?" He breathed deeply, then snapped off some words in rapid Arabic, a language he'd been trying for years to master. Though as a sculptor Rodni had no particular vision, by imbuing his work with an overlay of ethnicity (he was one-eighth Lebanese), he had managed to ford the distance between his lack of talent and a certain critical tolerance. The language and come-on were part of it. It also hid the fact that he never quite got anything anyone ever said to him.

"It comes down to this, Ben. The winds of change blow in many directions. But knowledge and the pursuit of it are not the same. Confuse the two and life will take you prisoner and pummel you against a large rock. Okay? Take care. Bye-bye."

Instantly, he was off and the phone handed back.

"Did you listen, Ben? I know you don't like him but he knows lots of things ordinary people like you and me don't."

I suddenly recalled Stella once telling me that she thought Rodni was a genius untouched, a naif who believed bookstores published the books they sold and who thought trees were the most important and evolved living organisms on Earth. He was fifty-four years old. Was it the child in him that held her? Or were the two of them both removed enough so they could remain separately adrift, yet happy for the company? Long ago I resolved to cut back on my deliberating about the past. Even if the present was just as unknowable, at least the material was fresher. This was no small consideration when you lived by yourself.

Stella was still talking energetically, a fact I gradually became aware of. She could no more understand me than I could carry on a conversation with a piece of custard pie, I thought.

"Do you know if Bistamante's is still open?" she asked. "Maybe they'll fly me out an order. Oh, Ben, I'll shut up now. It's late where you are. You'd better get some sleep. And it was real good hearing from you."

Gently, she hung up on me. And again, I was alone with the thoughts that I could not imagine communicating to anyone.

IV

WHEN I GOT back to my current hotel, I found the lobby empty and no one behind the front desk. Though it was not yet late afternoon, the place had taken on a deserted feel, as though all the guests had fled in my absence and now it was a just another out-of-season resort. It was so quiet that for an instant, I had the urge to trip the hotel's fire alarms and send the guests scurrying out of their rooms just to see who might be left. Instead I took my key from behind the desk and went upstairs.

What a strange encounter, I thought, as the elevator bore me upwards. Was the oversized man a typical case among the residents here? Or worse, was he the best of them? Looking at the outdated travel posters tacked up in the elevator (some at least a decade old, judging by the fashion), I began to wonder if the island could lay claim to anything resembling a national character. I recalled reading in my guidebook a little about the country's history and perusing a tourist brochure that detailed some of the native customs, broke down the currency conversions and gave the twenty-one essential declarations of an early Portuguese settler of Momo-Jima named de Basca. While there wasn't much to distinguish this island from the neighboring chain of Pacific outposts, I was struck in that it possessed a stranger passage than most of them.

I'd learned, for example, that the island first was inhabited by Chinese and Japanese fishermen around the third century AD. The British, who arrived to colonize it in the mid-1600s, renamed it Madigan's Island, apparently after a sailor who had tried to raise the St. George on the island's tallest peak but who instead tumbled several thousand feet to his death, becoming the island's first Western casualty. Fifty years later the island was then given to the French in a complicated settlement of English territories usurped because of the Portuguese war with the Dutch. But those intervening decades constituted the only extent to which Momo-Jima was ever considered valuable. From then on, it existed in constant impermanence, passing between the French and the English like an unwanted holiday gift, neither country desiring it but instead pawning it off whenever a goodwill occasion demanded. In the nineteenth century alone, the island had eight different foreign governorships and once even fell into Italian hands (accidentally, it appears). During World War II, the Japanese captured it and gave it back its former name but even the Imperial Army thought better of it and quickly abandoned it when events turned against them in the South Pacific. Following the war, Momo-Jima was temporarily assumed by United States, then handed back to France in apparent retaliation for a diplomatic snub. The matter was finally laid to rest when the French saw a public relations opportunity during a sticky time in the Pompidou presidency and gave Momo-Jima its independence in the late 1960s, against the wishes of the island's government and people.

(Apparently, the last straw for the French came with a fevered land craze that had swept Momo-Jima and ruined its economy, a debacle resulting from a geologist's "discovery" of vast fields of gemstones that lay beneath portions of the capital city.

Such a claim immediately set off a speculative boom that induced many in the white gentry to buy up the capital from the poorer native residents at three or four times the going rate. Assisting in such transactions was the geologist—his name was Cavalo—who acted both as an adviser to the most promising areas and who took a due percentage for his expertise. Based on his assessments, the ownership of the capital literally changed hands within weeks and planeloads of diamond experts soon began arriving from South Africa and Inner Siberia.

And of course, it was all a tremendous hoax. No diamonds or rubies or anything of value was ever mined, despite the vast bulldozing that took place for several months and which gutted most of the residential parts of the city. Cavolo was questioned, tentatively at first, then more insistently as the excavations turned up nothing. Soon afterwards, he and two local women disappeared forever from the island and many unsuccessful warrants were then issued over the years for their arrests.

Overnight, though, the bungle wrecked the fortunes of most of Momo-Jima's wealthier families. To this day, payments are still being made on the abandoned excavating equipment that lies pitted and rusting in fenced-off lots throughout the city and whole factions of families still refuse to speak to one another. Indeed, the only ones who made out were the mainly Japanese and Chinese residents who sold their land. Most of them fled Momo-Jima and settled in Brunei where they either bought high-rise apartments in the the old area of the capital city or became prosperous owners of sugar fields and cattle ranches. Today, there is a thriving second generation of several thousand Momo-Jimans in Brunei, with many having converted to Islam and now ensconced in the higher strata of government. One of them even stood recently as prime minister though he was forced to resign after being implicated in a scandal involving Macanese gamblers and members of the national jai alai team.

All this, of course, is according to my guidebook.)

With these thoughts busying themselves in my head, I locked myself in my room, drew the curtains and tried again to get some sleep. The silly, ragtag history of nations was none of my concern, and as for the character of the people here, I would find that out soon enough. A sense of superior contentment settled on me as I pulled a thick polyester blanket over myself and burrowed into the soft bed, inhaling the smell of the beach on my skin. I could now feel the accumulation of my travels and, turning off the air conditioning, I sank in for a good rest.

This time, it was the telephone that awoke me. In my deep slumber, I only gradually become aware of its tinkling noise, which sounded like the bell given to long-distance runners on their final lap. Slowly I stirred and picked up the phone that was bolted heavily to the nightstand, seemingly to discourage its use, and immediately heard a message that fully roused me. It emanated from the surly desk clerk who'd checked me in a few hours earlier.

"Mr. Inoue, please stay in your room," he said in a nasty and guttural voice. "The police are on their way up."

Abruptly the receiver was hung up without waiting for my response and then just as abruptly a man's voice came from the other side of my door.

"Mr. Inoue, time to open please! Momo-Jima Safety Enforcement."

In my surprise, and in complete darkness, all I could do was react. Quickly I scrambled out of bed and pulled on a pair of pants and looked for my glasses, which in my haste I knocked behind the nightstand. As I struggled to reach them and find a light switch, I was aware that my efforts were taking long seconds; I could feel the impatience of the man behind the door.

"Mr. Inoue, are you inside? Momo-Jima Safety," said the voice, now louder.

"Coming . . . one moment."

Still fumbling with my pants and with a thumbprint smeared over one of my lenses, I yanked open the door, but failed to notice that the door was still attached to its security chain. After I snatched it open, it rebounded shut with a terrific bang before I was able to unlatch it and finally see who was waiting for me.

To my added confusion, in the hallway stood a harmless-looking middle-aged man who greeted me agreeably, and with an expectation on his face that I would do the same. On his blue policeman's uniform was pinned a palm tree–shaped badge embossed with the words "Momo-Jima SE," and his name, Officer J. Entrade. A tiny pistol, slightly larger than a Derringer, was holstered on his hip.

"Mr. Inoue?" he said pleasantly. "Did they phone you from downstairs? I have here a warrant for your arrest. If you would look it over, sign it, and please come with me." In his hand, he held a folded pink piece of paper, which he offered to me in a friendly manner without pausing first to see if I'd object. His demeanor seemed more of an eager valet than a policeman's.

"Arrest? But I'm a tourist. I've only arrived this morning."

To my dismay, my voice, instead of sounding stolid and reassuring—and colored with humor at the obvious mix-up—sounded high-pitched and utterly panicked. No wonder the authorities come while their victims are asleep, I thought. Their visible distress only serves to confirm the need for the policeman's visit.

"Sorry, no mistake." The officer shook his head, almost as if in sympathy. "We received the call shortly after you checked in."

"For what? What did I do?"

"If you'll just read the ticket, it will show the charge."

Agitated, I glanced at the scrap of paper that had been put in my hand. On both sides, it was dense with obfuscation and printing that seemed like lines of tiny ants; it would take me several minutes to find and digest the information I was seeking. I also was aware that my hands were trembling and I tried harder to make sense of the words in front of me.

"I'm sorry for coming so late in the afternoon," said Entrade, by way of conversation as I fumbled with the citation, "but I was detained patrolling the boardwalk. Today is a half-holiday. It is National Education Day. All the schools are closed."

"Can't you just tell me what's wrong?"

"Actually, it's right here." Deftly, Entrade slipped the ticket from between my fingers, turned it over and slipped it back.

"At the top, the first section."

I looked again and saw that he was referring to a column titled "Common Tourist Infractions." It was a lengthy list that extended for several paragraphs and contained numerous clauses and subclauses.

"Provision B," said Entrade helpfully. "Right after Provision A."

I studied the paper some more and forced myself to focus my shaky attention. "Failure to pay outstanding hotel or inn charges," I finally read aloud.

"Oh no, no," he said hastily. "That would be presumptuous. It's the clause underneath."

"Failure to deposit full lodging charges on arrival."

"Yes, that's it," said Entrade happily, as if clearing up a disagreement over last year's World Cup winner or some other trifling matter. "It was the deposit in your case."

Like a concerned visitor, he then leaned his head into my room and glanced about, taking in my living arrangements.

"Shall we go? I would bring a jacket with you. The AC's been stuck on high and it's chilly in the back cells. Even during the day." He looked quizzically at me when I didn't respond right away.

"But I don't understand, what are 'full lodging charges'?" I burst out. "This is a complete misunderstanding. If they want me to pay the bill, I can settle this right now. You don't have to arrest me."

My panic suddenly had found its voice and it startled Entrade, who seemed only to be accustomed with meaningless chatter and ready cooperation. I saw him blanch, as if he were searching for words that were not in his possession. Emboldened, I continued, throwing a note of judiciousness into my delivery.

"The desk clerk didn't say anything about a deposit when I checked-in. If he had, I would've paid right away."

"But didn't you receive the notice of hotel rules and regulations?" inquired Entrade. "A yellow brochure? It's a standard handout. It's supposed to be given out at all hotels."

My heart sank. I recalled receiving the pamphlet—along with the one about the settler—and that I'd chucked it in the trash without a look. Officer Entrade read my reaction.

"Ah, yes. But you see, it's a standard rule and we enforce it vigorously. That is why it is Number B. It follows only Number A in manner of severity. We used to have a great problem with guests departing the island early and not paying their full amounts. The hotel associations now insist."

"But what if I pay now?"

"Oh, the amount already has been billed to your credit card, along with the standard non-compliance fee . . ."

I started to interrupt but Entrade held up one hand and with the other lightly touched his tiny gun.

"I'm sorry for the disturbance, but still I must take you into custody. I've no choice. It's the standard procedure. But trust me, it should be resolved quickly."

At these words, I shivered. Anytime one hears the word "custody" as applied to himself, it is an instant and bottomless sensation.

I made one more appeal.

"Really, can't we settle this here? I really think there's been a misunderstanding. I'm not trying to avoid anything."

"I'm sorry, Mr. Inoue. This is a police matter now. Do you have everything you need?"

I stood speechless for a moment, then numbingly went back into my room for my shoes, wallet, passport and hotel key, resigned now to the absurd circumstances and dismissing all possibilities of any overt action that might elevate me above them. Rage, if and when I could locate it, would have to be directed another time at other people.

Officer Entrade made small noises of sorrow as I gathered my things. It occurred to me that he would make a good therapist or repossessions specialist. In his duties he easily adopted a genuinely pained expression that neutralized the feelings of the injured party.

Indeed, as I stepped into the hall, another look of concern crossed his face.

"But don't you have a jacket?" he said. "Never mind the AC, at night the cells are cold all by themselves."

I shook my head sullenly. Officer Entrade closed off the hotel room behind me and took out a small walkie-talkie from his back pocket and spoke into it.

"This is Patrol 44-Diamond. I'm at the hotel and will be coming in with the prisoner. About ten minutes. Can you bring up a jacket for him? Perhaps the green one with the gray hood. He doesn't seem to have one."

The police desk responded back, congratulating Entrade on his safe arrest before spitting out something incomprehensible over the radio static.

Turning to me, Entrade beamed at the communique which obviously had gone in his favor and then spoke pleasantly some more.

"It's no problem with the jacket, Mr. Inoue. They're bringing it up right now. In fact, they said they're waiting for you."

V

I wish I knew what causes me to become so helpless in situations like these. Yes, I could have resisted and put up a fight but a sense of sheer futility always overcomes me just when I most need the lash of purposeful outrage. In a moment, I seem to fully understand all the long-term implications of my situation and thus am perfectly willing to quit my short-term struggling because of it. Besides, on the occasions when my irregular anger does arise, it never does me any good; usually it erupts over some generalized, world-engulfed condition in which I am incapable of action, anyway (say, religious intolerance or ethnic warfare), rather than any situation at hand. As a result, I've found it better to try and avoid outrage altogether.

Or perhaps it's just a greater realization that dawns on me. Caught in the grip of unforeseen events, I often recall my journalistic experiences and the thousands of situations I have been privy to and tried to record. From them, I've learned that it occasionally falls on all of us to be prodded forth when we least deserve it and to be made public for others' comment and analyses. Perhaps from this we learn more of what it is like to be ourselves and how then to suffer our individual destinies.

This awareness, of course, comes afterward. In the immediate flush of such experiences, nothing at all gives comfort or makes sense and one's primary intention is only to learn the new codes of conduct: I have to walk ahead now but only one step, not two. I can ask to use the bathroom but I likely won't go alone. I can ask for a cigarette if the other person smokes, etc. As it was now with me. With my hands manacled in full frontal view, I was escorted through the lobby that now was congested with gawking German tourists, helped into a police Jeep parked curbside, and taken on a brief but windswept ride into the dilapidated town center. I thus emerged on the other end with my handcuffs and exploded hair looking something on the order of a distempered prophet, or at the very least, an obvious sociopath.

Officer Entrade helped me from the Jeep and into the grimy station, which, like his uniform, was colored a bright tropical blue. Inside, there was only one other officer and a middle-aged woman with a red face who sat behind a row of potted plants at a desk marked "Civilian Volunteer." They interrupted their conversation to smile and nod at me as I was led through the room and down another hallway—this one a narrow passage with high ceilings— finally to my cell where another officer with a too-large cap and a smear of purple chalk dust on his shirt waited for us.

"Here we are," said Entrade. "And they've brought you your jacket."

With a slight push from behind, I was entered into the cell and the grated door swung shut. Before me was a plywood cot on which lay a torn jacket spraying filthy gray down. The room was cold and infected with a sour fungal smell and faint sunlight struggled to penetrate a cloudy plexiglass window. A busy halo of green flies circled overhead. Faced with this, I then did what every actor in every standard prison drama does—I turned around, grasped the bars and looked out. In front of me was the opposite wall of the dingy corridor.

But then a voice spoke up quickly behind me.

"Ah, thank you, George Baker, for the company."

I turned and saw with intense dismay the large, fleshy man whom I'd spoken to (or rather, who had spoken to me) on the beach. He still had on his tan suit and as before, he thrust out his right hand as if I was about to run away from him. As he strode across the cell, I also saw he had a pronounced limp on his left side.

"We meet again, as I thought we might," he said as he assaulted me anew. "It's Trevor MacGower, recall?"

I again took his moist hand and this time felt the presence of at least two rings on his fat fingers. After a moment, I tried to release myself from his grip but he clung onto my hand, wringing it continually as if he was trying to transmit some of his goodwill to me. Standing so close to him, I could smell the acrid and powerful odor of sweat wafting about him.

"Yes, I recall," I said.

"And you're Inoue, right? From the States, I'd guessed, though not a typical one."

"That's right," I said, only catching his meaning after a few seconds.

"Well, welcome." He extended one arm as if showing off the expanse of the cell. "Funny that we see each other here, but it's an opportunity as well. Think of this as seeing the side of things you rarely visit. Before you're back on shore tomorrow with all the other tourists. They won't know what they've missed."

"Really."

Trevor nodded his head vigorously.

"I've always learned more about countries from their jails than from their tourist sites," he said. "The soul of a nation lies in its opposition. Perhaps that's even a saying."

"I suppose," I said as dryly I could, and this time he got my irony and finally let go of my hand.

"Really, it's not to worry. Whatever you've been arrested for can't be that much or that expensive. Forgive us, but these minor infractions are the lifeblood of small nations like ours. For years, tourist violations were our greatest source of GNP. It would be unusual if you didn't contribute in some way during your stay here."

He looked at my slyly. "What did you do?"

On his face I saw the rising glow of anticipation, as if he was about to hear the story of an ironic misdeed or a cosmic mishap that should not have jail as its final result. It was an oddly gluttonous appeal with no overt show of any sympathy.

"I didn't pay the hotel bill when I checked in."

Trevor's face turned a dark blotch and he took a step back from me as if I had just developed a contagion.

"Oh, that is very serious," he said in a low voice. "Very serious. You should be careful."

"I'm been told that."

But now I said this as coldly as I could. Hearing my crime, as it were, mentioned again in such somber tones stirred in me a welter of resentment. Stuck in dirty confinement, I felt my allowances thinning for the absurd native customs, none of which seemed to exhibit any rationality. Were the guard to open the door, I thought, I just might push past him and make a run for it. Were these the first inklings of the criminal mind?

"Even though I have paid the bill."

"Oh, I am sure of it," said Trevor. "Not doubting it for a moment. But the hoteliers and tourist associations regard this violation with great importance. I am a member of the island's main travelers organization and can attest to their vigilance. They've never wavered in their support of this law. It ensures the stability of the tourist industry. But as I'm running for president, I promise to give the matter full reconsideration when I take office."

He remained utterly serious and now I was astonished. For I believed him at once. Not only did his face have the certitude of someone not quite of this world, but he also spoke quite unaffectedly, as if what he told me was only a minor fact that I hadn't been apprised of.

Likewise, my reporter's intuition to high folly confirmed my belief. Grand desires often lurk within the most unremarkable of men; turning their focus inward, they neglect the fact of how they must appear to the rest of world as they pursue their deepest needs. Indeed, more unbelievable to me was that the flimsy island would actually undergo the ritual of electing someone to lead it.

At any rate, I took him at face value, meaning that I believed what he said and then placed it in its proper low regard.

"Do they usually arrest presidential candidates here?" I asked.

Trevor shrugged. "Another small matter. It should be cleared up by this evening."

"That's what I've been told."

"In my case, I have assurances." His tone became imperious as if he was aware of the odd situation and wanted to brazen out any suspicions I had of him. But his anxiety was misplaced. As I said, I trusted in the genuineness of his lucid perversity.

"My brother is the one who had me arrested," he said finally. "After Grandmama's estate hears of it, they'll release me."

"Your brother? What did you do?"

At this, Trevor drew himself up as best he could.

"I was fighting for the betterment of our nation. Campaigning for the chance to rebuild our society along worthier lines."

I said nothing, merely nodded.

"My brother is currently vice president and is running against me," he went on. "He has done this on occasion when the newspaper surveys show that I am more popular. This time the charge was conspiracy to incite a disturbance. But I was merely passing out fliers to drivers along the Roka-dori. They all were eager to receive them."

"Your brother is the vice president? Here?" My astonishment returned. "When is the election?"

"Three and a half weeks. I have great hopes this time. I'm calling for the privatization of all military, education, and relief services, the building of an international arena for sporting and entertainment events, and legislating driving on the left-hand side of the road after a three-month trial period. These measures will finally pull us into the modern times. 'Now's The Hour for Trevor Mac-Gower'. Surely you've seen my signs."

"Have you run before?"

"Twice. Once I was defeated by inexperience while the second time I was the subject of false criticism by the island cleric, Rector Froines. He has since changed his opinion and now is quite active on my behalf. Perhaps you've heard one of his speeches praising me?"

"I only arrived today."

"Oh yes, of course."

At this, Trevor went quiet. Perhaps the fact that I had been on the island nearly four hours but still had not heard of him was an indication that his bid for office might again be doomed to the familiar scrap heap of misfortune. Strong drives likely are balanced by equally strong states of emotional disorder, I thought, and I decided to leave him alone as he now began to brood, limping back to his bed and sitting moodily in his out-of-date suit. In this manner, he reminded me of a petulant toddler engulfed by the passage of heavy and current emotions. But after several minutes, his expression cleared and he perked up again to address me.

"And what do you do?" he asked in a manner that was more a command than a question. "You're from the States, you said."

As best as I could, I explained my career to him. Given the peculiarities of my freelance existence, I spoke merely to the facts of various employers and only touched upon the psychological dimensions of my choices. Truthfully, though, those details, through repetition over the years to acquaintances, occasional psychologists, and second and third dates, had begun to bore me as well. Whatever insight I had been able to give to others because of my experiences had long ago dried up or simply seemed meaningless. Perhaps that was the real reason I neglected my past now.

Yet Trevor seemed interested after I'd finished.

"It all sounds rather fascinating," he said. "In many ways, though I have never been a writer, our work seems very similar. Frequently, I am assailed by journalists and have wondered what they are thinking as they pelt me with their supposedly meaningful queries. Now I have a better idea. It is quite close to what I do."

"What do you mean?"

I didn't want to ask the question—for it would invite more conversation—but in my self-acting reporter's way it slipped out of its own accord.

"As a journalist, your success depends on your ability to tell the public a believable story," he answered. "Every day, a new narrative assembled from the daily commonalties. Thousands of events, but only a handful that can truly satisfy the desires of readers. It's your job to discern the public's taste for them."

I could see Trevor's face turning crimson from excitement and the sudden assumption of a deep agreement between us, and he began speaking in a raised voice.

"A politician is nothing but a story himself, a plot with a beginning, middle, and end. If people are going to support him, they need to be interested in his adventures and experiences. In this way, they feel linked with his cause and they endorse him with their innermost feelings. But first, like a journalist, a politician must have his believable story, otherwise his is just another voice. In the end, we are both captives to the public's imagination."

I had not heard of this way of thinking before but it did not seem implausible to me. In fact, considering it, it seemed to me that all the successful candidates I'd covered possessed this quality. For them, success depended upon first gauging the public's appetite for the story it wanted to hear, then developing the charisma and forthrightness to deliver it (the effect was similar to watching a hologram materialize). I had tried to relate this basic phenomenon many times in various political assignments but the finer points always had been ground up and discarded by my editors.

"And what story are you proposing?" I asked politely. "Is it simply that you're against your brother?"

"In this, I have struggled to find myself," Trevor admitted. "Stanley always has been the more inventive one. It is because he is younger and had to distinguish himself from me that he has enjoyed this advantage. It is an arbitrary privilege but nevertheless a real one." He looked at me closely.

"Currently, I have no story. And the election is just days away. It has been extremely frustrating. Even my closest advisors have been unable to fully understand my aims."

He said this in a manner that made me distinctly uncomfortable. In that moment I felt he'd made another assumption, one not just about me but one that now included me. A small knot of worry flared up in my chest.

"But you might understand," he said intently. "You tell stories for a living. You must know exactly what I need."

"Me? I doubt it. I know nothing about the politics here."

I said this humorously to try and offset the making of any overture. When I was a full-time reporter, there were many people who become attached to me for what they thought I could do for them, given my access to the media. Usually, these types only lacked for a coherent sense of principle or reason.

"The situation here is like any other," Trevor insisted. "There is nothing new or unnatural that you wouldn't find in America. In this, we are just as pragmatic about things as you are. Perhaps more so because we are smaller." Here he stopped and looked past me as though recognizing his own implication in what he had just said. I noticed that when he brooded, his eyebrows pinched together to form a fleshy, upside-down V.

"I would like to propose that you come work with me," he said decisively. "As soon as possible, to manage the rest of my campaign. There isn't time to be wasted."

"Work? But I'm a tourist. I'm only here a few days." Now my voice could not hide its incredulity. Though I had expected an offer, to hear him say it aloud was ludicrous.

"A place with my operation. Assisting with strategy and vision. I'm down to my final straws and this is my last opportunity. To fail twice signifies to voters you are a serious and dogged man. But to fail three times is saying that you don't know when to quit. It is to appear a fool. So I cannot lose now." He added in a low voice: "I'm willing to pay well."

"But I'm on vacation. I don't want a job."

"Not a job but a position of command. Marshalling the strength and direction of an entire campaign. A machine at your fingertips."

"But I have no experience in politics . . . I'm a journalist. And I'm leaving in a couple of weeks. Twelve days, in fact."

"This is a rare opportunity, Ben. Your expertise is quite valuable. It wouldn't do to leave it unused. You could affect the destinies of thousands."

"I write stories for a living, I don't make them up. And I've never done anything political in my life. I'm not sure I could."

"Momo-Jima is strategically placed. It is a coming power center of the Pacific Rim. Already, our sapodillas have attracted the world's attention. In years, your grandchildren will be reading stories about you. Perhaps they will be here, as well. Ho Chi Minh was once a journalist, too, I recall."

I suddenly remembered Minh being a chef's assistant, not a reporter, but dismissed the thought of correcting him.

"Your offer is generous," I said, "but really, it's impossible. I'm not at all qualified for the job and besides, I'm only here for a short time. I leave on the twentieth."

At this, Trevor said nothing. Instead, his eyes narrowed and he sighed disgruntledly as if he was to impart a reluctant truth. Something in his manner shifted as well, and as he faced me, I suddenly felt an adversarial air descending between us. When he spoke, too, his voice seemed gruffer and less amenable.

"You are naturally free to think what you'd like," he said sternly, "but when you leave and when you think you'll be leaving may be quite different matters. It's not always so easy. Sometimes the arrangements can be more difficult than you imagine."

"What do you mean by that?"

"Nothing. Only that there's no telling when you'll be released. Tonight possibly, or maybe even in a week. I've known several who've had your difficulty. Your charge is not taken so lightly here. And you are, after all, a tourist."

"But I can't stay locked up for a bill I've already paid," I said, struggling to keep my composure against the mounting irrationality of his words. "They can't keep me indefinitely."

"And on what do you base your assumptions? Are you in a position to leave?"

Again, Trevor waved one arm around the fetid bounds of the cell. This time, though, the gesture was done savagely to convey a different meaning of confinement. And when he spoke, it was in a charged voice.

"Have they gotten you a lawyer? Have you been told of what might happen to you? Do you even know how many counts are against you?"

His vehemence startled me; I had not expected to feel such sudden force from him. Until now, I thought him oppressive but fully capable of being fended off. But what he was saying now also was true.

"Have they given you a phone call?" he continued, "or the chance to speak with anyone? Do you have a court date? Is the consulate even aware of you?

"Where is the American consulate here?" I asked, chagrined that it hadn't occurred to me.

"There isn't one," he replied with satisfaction. "The nearest diplomatic office is in Ryonama-Jima, four hundred miles away. But the posting is vacant and the office manager has been covering the duties. But he's a local hire and speaks only Chamorro with a little Korean. His job is to replace lost passports. He won't help you."

He paused. "So as you can see, your release is hardly crossing anyone's mind."

His words struck me with the force of physical blows. I now saw how easily I had fallen victim to my own beliefs as to the legal processes in an English-speaking nation. For the second time in under an hour, I felt overwhelmed and helpless. Now it was my turn to sit heavily on the cot and suffer my feelings. Pulling the dirty jacket over me, I tried to think of what other authorities might come to my aid. I doubted whether even the Red Cross would deign to intercede in this desolated fragment, or figment, of the world. Perhaps somehow I could smuggle out a letter . . .

Recognizing the effect he'd had upon me, Trevor was silent for several moments, holding himself away in a far corner of the cell. However, when he spoke again, I could sense another shift in his demeanor. Now his voice had a patrician tone, much like the manner of someone explaining the rules of a simple board game, even if what he had to say did not match the character of such words.

"Now that he's had me arrested, Stanley owes me back," he said. "It's the usual course of things and besides, Grandmama's attorneys will see to it. They don't want the trouble. But given his position, I could ask that he intervene in your circumstances. Both in your favor or against."

My mouth went dry. I had never before been the victim of a blackmail (and that was the word that immediately sprang to mind), though I had written about them several times. Frantically, I tried to recall the details of those long-ago stories as if they might help me now but the only thing I remembered was how inexorably the victims had clung to their personal shame, even though most of the blackmailed acts—adultery, small financial crime, false personal histories—were illicities routinely committed by millions of others. That was what the blackmailers always banked on, I learned. Not the indecent act but the self-identity of their victims.

But as I struggled to reflect on this, another more curious thought came to me and suddenly I found myself swimming in a personal dilemma that I had been conceiving and reconceiving for myself for some time. Simply put, I was now of an age where I was defined more by the things I could not do than by what I could. Invariably, at some point during the day a new impossibility would occur to me and at these times I saw myself drifting farther and farther past the meridian that divided my youth and its evolution from that of my age and decline. And indeed, not only had I accomplished little of what I had envisioned for myself as a driven youth (for I had dreamed quite hard then) but the few matters over which I now did have dominion seemed pitiable, if not laughable.

Likewise, it also seemed that for my entire last decade, I'd accommodated myself to these limitations and that this was the real reason I worked as a freelancer. Alone, my only specter was myself, with my only standards of comparison those dredged from personal experience. Maybe it was true, as my ex-wife once said to me, that I carried in me the seeds of an artist's temperament and that this was what accounted for my self-imposed isolation (or was it the other way around?). I also knew, and abided by, the Latin proverb I'd encountered in my youth: *Qui, perd perche*. An unsuccessful man always offends.

But there also is a price to pay for setting yourself off from the world and ignoring its standards, I knew, and that is the courting of purposelessness that comes when you are your only reference. As it was now with me. For awhile my routines had seemed like the backdrop to existence rather than the thing itself; in the quieter moments of my day, I felt I was able to acknowledge the difference (or if I couldn't, I at least felt the absence of something better for myself). Was ambivalence and loss—that is, the ability to discard one's most valuable wishes without any desire to reclaim them—really a sign of personal evolution?

And then suddenly the private image of the dead man swinging from an old hotel fixture came back to me, startling and terrifying in its futile eloquence. He too had kept his own lonely vigil. To what point? I wondered. To what end did his seclusion carry him?

So it was with this kind of thinking filling my head, and wrapped in a filthy torn jacket and sitting on a thin jail mattress that I considered my unlucky options some more and stood to answer Trevor, quietly bearing in mind some words I'd read just hours earlier:

"Never look to the past. Nothing's there" (Orozco de Basca—Declaration #4).

VI

For a day, I enjoyed myself. After my release from jail, I made plodding visits to the several negligible sights that made for the tourist's agenda in Momo-Jima. In one afternoon, I visited an ancient fish processing plant (still capable of churning out two tons of fish emulsion per day even though it was built in 1923); the island's tallest structure, a thirteen-story television tower that was topped by an enormous replica of the island's native bird, the Guanche; and then the rather subdued Orozco de Basca memorial, which featured a life-size figure of him made from carved cork. Later that evening, I hired a moko-moko driver to take me on a long coastal trip to survey the rest of the island's shoreline while I downed bottle after bottle of the native beer. Perhaps I surmised that this day might be my last run of freedom for awhile and I wanted to take advantage.

But to my surprise, when I got back late to my hotel there were no messages or communiqués waiting for me. Stripping off my dirty clothes, and rummaging for aspirins to circumvent any incipient hangovers, I allowed myself to briefly wonder if I simply had been a passing fancy that was thought better of and thus was released from duty. Perhaps I had even been forgotten altogether. These were pleasant thoughts to indulge in even though I knew they were highly unlikely given Trevor's levels of desperation and need. Moreover, the longer I entertained them, the more depressing they became since they confirmed that I now bore the perspective of an indentured employee, one always mindful of my employer's demands. Even a bout of unworried sleep—which I had been envisioning on the dark silent ride back to the hotel—technically was not mine to freely enjoy. This realization was my final demoralization of the day and it left me feeling fully dispirited. Flopping down on the bed, I turned off the light and buried my head in the pillow to get what rest I could before what I presumed was to be a long and early day. But it was quite awhile before I could convince myself to fall asleep and the sleep I did get seemed hardly worth the effort.

The telephone rang at six a.m. just as the early sunlight was peering into my room. I picked up the receiver and Trevor immediately began speaking in my ear as if we already were deep in conversation.

"Ben, I've had many new thoughts since we spoke. Did you read the notices of my speeches? The piece in the *News Review* was practically a raver. The *Morning Gleaner* has been kind, too."

I replied as best I could despite now feeling the effects of the many beers I'd had, as well as having so far avoided any of the island's newspapers, several of which I'd cursorily examined and found to be filled mostly with cheap ads, wire stories on celebrities, and astrology columns. Thus, I not only had missed both the *Review* and *Gleaner* pieces but, as Trevor went on, equally adulatory stories in the *Avoucher*, the *Sun and Stars*, and the *Eastern Edifier*.

"I think we've found our way," he exulted. "I've called a session at eight to capitalize. It's also a chance to introduce you. How about 'Take a Stand for the Other Brother' or 'Pull the Lever for Trevor' as slogans? I'll send Wilkie to pick you up. We're usually informal but perhaps you might want to dress up at first."

I began another reply but before I could get out the words, Trevor had rung off, gone already to other worlds and oblivious to the one he had just left behind. Glumly, it occurred to me that the inexorable personality I'd been witnessing might only be a glimmer of an even more overabundant willfulness. So far, his sense of himself had not abated for a moment in my presence.

Shakily, I made my way to the shower, turned it on full-force and lay steaming for several minutes, trying to comprehend and alleviate my dread. This was not typical trouble, I thought, both in its complexity and location. Usually I have found that the smaller the authority, the more baroque and oppressive are its restrictions. And Momo-Jima was the smallest place I had ever been to (and Trevor the most insecure employer). I could not even begin to imagine what might be expected of me here, much less what I would have to do to be successful at it.

Stepping out of the tub, I then examined myself in the mirror. Even through the steam, I could identify several new lines emerging around my mouth, forehead, and eyes. The reprimand of all my days, I thought, the outer finally revealing the inner as it eventually does. Mindful of this, I wondered if this, at last, was what ultimately defined people—not what they did or who they were, but what they had to give in to.

Not wishing to linger on the thought, I changed and went down to the lobby for the local papers. In them—between the horoscopes and the inflated dramas of local crimes—I found that Trevor was being only half truthful. The story in the *News Review* was quietly favorable but the *Morning Gleaner* piece was one long screed against his candidacy. Some of it was a less-than-overt type of scorn but the essential insult of the article was plain. I tore both stories from the paper, put them aside and committed to memory the name of the *Gleaner* reporter: R. S. Bando.

I was just finishing up a longish account on the elections in the *Edifier* (which, despite Trevor's assertion of support, did not mention him at all) when there was a sound at the door. A short rap to be polite and then a longer knock to be heard. I rose and opened the door to a squat man of Trevor's age with full black hair, an ugly pug's face, and the kind but wary eyes often seen on shortish men. He was dressed formally in an old brown suit and held himself back, but as with only a few people I have met in my life, I found myself taking an immediate sympathy to him. He seemed to be someone resigned to a substandard position in life owing to the discrepancy between his irregular appearance and what looked to be his seeming intelligence and sensitivity—an event that, of course, was not lost on him. Using both hands, he awkwardly gripped an oversized burgundy briefcase.

"Good morning," he said deferentially. "You're Mr. Inoue? I'm Wilkie."

I held the door open wider but he didn't respond. Instead, he solemnly handed me the attaché, which looked as if it had just been purchased a few moments before.

"This is for you from Mr. MacGower," he said.

"Thank you," I said, taking the briefcase, which was made of a pebble-grain leather and surprisingly heavy. "Please, come in."

He shook his head.

"If you don't mind, we're just a bit late. Traffic is standing on the Kunobasho-dori. They're building a new archway at Grande Place to replace the one that collapsed during the Independence Day celebration. It's a terrible mess. We've just enough time to make it back across town."

Like the police officer before him, Wilkie then waited in the hall while I gathered my effects, which this time included a tape recorder, a notebook, and the recent clippings about Trevor. I also made sure to hide in my suitcase the cache of coconut candies that I'd stolen from the bowl in the lobby and to stuff the newspapers in an empty drawer.

It was a long and congested ride to Trevor's, during which we traveled through several neighborhoods that took us farther and farther from what I perceived to be the center of the city. In the backseat of the car—an ancient Renault diesel that throbbed heavily whenever we stopped—I examined the briefcase, wondering if it were mine to keep or whether it was just on loan to me for the assignment. It was of quality issue and had a gold, four-numbered combination lock at the handle along with old-fashioned brass welts to protect its corners. Back home, I estimated, it might cost several hundred dollars.

Glancing at me in the rearview mirror, Wilkie nodded that I should open it. Inside, I found the red satin plush was filled with an array of office items, including a stapler, a clutch of ballpoint pens and markers, a wrapped bundle of notepads, a blank financial ledger, and a hardback dictionary. There also were a dozen file folders labeled with subjects such as, "Wardrobe and Appearance," "Phrases to Remember," "Advice on Radio Interviews" and "Foods to Order/Avoid." I took the newspaper clippings from my pocket and put them in the folder marked, "Negative Press," surprised that Trevor's egoism had permitted him to consider such a file.

I was wondering about the purpose of another folder entitled, "Lunch Topics: The Great Barrier Reef" when the old car ground to a halt and Wilkie switched off the engine.

I saw we had parked in front of a decrepit tan bungalow. Conceivably, it might have once been the best house in the ramshackle neighborhood but that was another generation and now it had become like the rest—a sad structure whose only features were the rotting wood sides typical of uncared-for tropical homes, a front yard ablaze with a bright purple flower, and inside the yard, a plastic box filled with several dingy candelabras. On the windows was some white bunting, a large cardboard sign that read, "MacGower for President," a number of campaign stickers, and another sign that announced, "Light Fixtures Sale."

The presidential candidate was waiting for us on the porch, holding a large, clear pitcher of yellow juice. With one hand he acknowledged us, then abruptly disappeared inside.

Wilkie ran up to the house and opened the door for me.

"Straight through, Mr. Inoue."

Self-consciously gripping my new briefcase, I followed Trevor's trail. He had waited for me in the gloomy entrance and as we walked through the house, he paused to describe the function of each room we passed.

"This is my library and conference room," he said, ushering me past a bare living room and foyer. "The rear door opens to the strategy room. It has three computers, four televisions, and two cameras. I practice my public speaking there. The videotape is cruel but honest."

Exiting from the dark house, we then emerged onto a sunny back porch that looked out on an unkempt backyard bordered by wild shrubbery and several varieties of fruit trees. Waiting for us at a table laden with breads and fresh-cut fruits was a blunt-faced older woman in a green peasant skirt and a large police whistle about her neck, and a short man with wire glasses and an anxious expression. There also was a nude rotund man sitting at the far end. He nodded cheerfully to me.

"This is my advisory committee," said Trevor. "They have been with me for every election, through good weather and bad. This is Mrs. Murazami and Mr. Cecilia. Mrs. Murazami is my general secretary and Mr. Cecilia is my chief financial aide. But they began as simple volunteers just like you. And Mr. Botolph is my official shouter."

He indicated the naked man, who bounded up to shake my hand. I saw that despite the fact he was nude, he had on high-top basketball sneakers and thick white socks.

"Thank you for joining us," he said to me.

"What is an official shouter?" I asked politely, keeping my eyes fixed on his face.

"The stirrer of crowds, the mover of masses," said Trevor, before the naked man could respond. "His is a most important function in our efforts. The shouter is the one who transforms the energy of the people into a movement."

As if on cue, the nude man then began chanting Trevor's name in a booming, thunderous voice that rose out of the scrabbly backyard and far out in the world beyond. Pleased with himself, he continued for several moments before Trevor indicated for him to stop.

"To see Mr. Botolph with a crowd is like a miracle," he said approvingly. "I have seldom seen such public excitement. Unfortunately, Mr. Botolph's choice of lifestyle has limited his effectiveness but I am on the verge of changing his views."

"It has been my ambition since I was a child," said Mr. Botolph proudly. Unselfconsciously, he began to thump his chest as if clearing it of congestion. "I keep myself like an athlete."

As if to prove his point, he then reached down and performed ten toe touches. For a portly man, he was surprisingly agile.

"I have a natural lifestyle," he boasted. "I eat only what comes from the earth, preferably our native fruits, such as the sapodilla. I eat ten a day for my circulation. It is the secret to my energy. That, and living unencumbered, next to the sun."

Trevor nodded vigorously.

"He is right to credit them," he said. "More first-grade sapodillas are grown per acre here than anywhere, and our latex is found in the most significant chewing gums. Soon we will begin exporting them to the world. It will be our avenue to esteem, like the Japanese and their radios. If it weren't for the local unions, our fruits would be well-known already."

"The unions?" I asked.

"They wish to tightly control our production so our exports may cost more on the world's markets," he said bitterly. "They fail to recognize the overall delicacy of the global competition in which we are engaged. They are a true hindrance to our progress as a nation. No wonder they oppose me."

"It is to be expected," grunted Mr. Botolph, who had dropped to the ground and now commenced a series of push-ups. "But at least you have the growers behind you. They know what you stand for."

"Yes, it is thanks to them that I enjoy the support I do, even if sometimes I wonder if I can afford such approval," said Trevor, suddenly glum. "One voter told me that one word from them is like fifty from my enemies. They have not fully regained their reputation since the Bandicoot Troubles."

I turned to Mr. Cecilia.

"Several years ago, the growers' league introduced bandicoots to regulate the native pests," he explained. "Only they now have bred so much that they are a pestilence and have gone on to eat many of our crops and domestic pets. The growers have found little favor since, though their leader, Rector Froines, is affiliated with us. In fact, some people, when they wish to be disrespectful, draw him with a bandicoot's face."

He said this last part solemnly as if to stress the seriousness of the religious offense. Mr. Botolph, in particular, looked pained. Or perhaps it was from his routine, which he was continuing to attack with one hand.

"It doesn't sound like a very nice gesture," I offered.

"Truly, it is not to be mentioned," said Mr. Cecilia gently, as if shepherding the subject onto a more polite plane. "But that is often the way with those who have no direction in things. They seek out others on whom to acquire their stature."

He pushed a bowl of odd-looking brown fruit toward me, changing the subject.

"Would you like to try one, Mr. Inoue?" he asked. "These are delicious and just ready to eat."

Uncertainly, I picked up one of apple-sized fruits and bit into it. The flesh was firm but the taste of the pulp was instantly sweet and dense with sugar, much like a compacted piece of cotton candy. But sugar, or sweetness of any kind, is a taste I rarely seek out since it easily becomes overpowering for me and often induces a temporary, but piercing, toothache. Already, I could feel my fillings start to ache.

I put the fruit down and reached for a glass of water, trying to preserve the neutral look on my face, which I aware was being searched for a reaction.

"It's just like I thought it would be," I managed to say.

VII

"We don't have a history of independent elections, you know," Trevor said ruefully. We were back in the house now, sitting inside the dark and stuffy strategy room where all three televisions played silently and Mr. Cecilia was trying unsuccessfully to open a safe containing the campaign funds. "The legacy is a new one. I remember voting in my first presidential election when I was twenty-nine. I said to myself, 'If a man can vote, a man can run,' and I've been in the midst ever since. Care for a vitamin?"

He offered me a blue porcelain bowl filled with a number of foil-wrapped pellets, but I shook my head. Trevor took a handful, meticulously unwrapped them and laid them on his armrest within easy reach, and continued.

"We belonged to the French until we finally gained our freedom in 1968. But it was embarrassing for us. For years, they had tried to get rid of us and because we didn't know any other way, we clung to them. They even built a new airport here, saying tourists would come and hoping we would become independent from it. But after that didn't happen, the Pompidou government said it was time for us to grow up and leave. I remember watching his speech on television that day as a young man."

"It must have been very sad."

Trevor waved it off.

"It was but it doesn't matter. The moment was right for us to assert ourselves. By then, we'd had some political demonstrations and our first premonitions of destiny. Within a few years, we had broken off all ties with them."

He stopped to eat two of the vitamins.

"Now everyone sees that our long association crippled us greatly. Their shadow was a dark and terrible one. Almost as bad as what the Americans have done in their countries."

Trevor stopped.

"You're not sensitive about it, are you?"

"Not at all," I said honestly.

"Fine for you then."

He continued: "Still, for a long time, our prospects were bleak. Once our initial pride of freedom ran dry, there was little to sustain us. We attempted to develop an agricultural base, but on the advice of the farming minister most of the island was planted in cinnamon and after the soil became waterlogged, we lost the entire yield. We then painted one of our beaches as a tourist attraction but that was in a summer of much political unrest and no one traveled. We even became anti-American for a few years hoping for an invasion but none came . . . probably because we had no strongman to topple. And by the time we decided on one, it was too late and your administration had changed. I won't bore you with how we've excavated the capital looking for diamonds."

Over Trevor's head, I saw on one of the televisions a man with a spun white beard gesticulating theatrically at a young woman. He seemed to have the character of a yapping terrier. Fearing my distraction if it continued, I asked Mrs. Murazami to switch it off.

"How did things change?" I asked politely.

"They haven't, not yet," said Trevor bitterly. "Simply, we've just gotten by. It's been a matter of surviving, not thriving."

"The past governments have been reluctant to address the real needs of the people and establish a viable future," interrupted Mr. Cecilia, who had given up on the safe and who now was wrapping stacks of pennies in brown paper cylinders. "We have been greatly disappointed many times."

At this, Trevor nodded.

"It's long overdue to be rid of them and their ways. We are now seeking the chance to remake our nation."

"Who has been in power?"

"Mostly the Higher Standards party," said Trevor. "They have occupied the presidency for over ten years. First by a man named Zavala, then by Stanley, then by Zavala again. Zavala has said he will resign this year, so it is Stanley's turn once more."

In my notebook, I wrote down these facts, as well as the name of Trevor's party, "The Faultless Future," which had appeared in smaller lettering under his name on the handful of posters around town. I still didn't know what had prevented the country from attaining its seemingly modest goals of self-sufficiency, nor did I have a sense for what were the issues, if any, that divided its population. But I also got the feeling that to ask Trevor these questions now would be useless. Better to concentrate on the narrow spectrum of phenomena in front of me than to engage in unintelligible matters that I could not encompass, I thought. I thus continued in my usual reporter's mode—that is, to carry on with questions until the appearance of some useful answers.

"On what issues do you differ with Stanley?" I asked.

"We have no points in common other than genealogy," said Trevor crossly. "I am sometimes astonished that we are related. Needless to say, he has opposed all my propositions and naturally, he has refused to debate me on my views. His campaign is founded in insecurity and fear. Of course, it is in his personality, as well."

"Yes, but what about his proposals?"

"He has none, at least none worthwhile. To hear him speak is to be instructed in delusion. What he says sounds reasonable until you listen closer. Then it is nothing but a proposition for anarchy."

"Mr. MacGower is right," Mrs. Murazami said loudly, speaking for the first time all afternoon. "I've heard his suggestions often but each time I've had to shut my ears. He has a wayward temperament. He needs more fresh air."

"But," I interrupted persistently, throwing a note of implacability into my voice, "what can you tell me about his campaign? What has he done in office? Surely he's accomplished something."

At this, there was a reluctant silence that lasted several moments. Finally, a tight-lipped Trevor began mumbling, parsing out his words as if they were dollar bills.

"Of course, every once in a while he has a decent notion. At heart he might be a decent man. But he has never been right for our nation. He has a strong wish to impose his way. Once his manner nearly caused us a revolution."

"Revolution?" I was surprised. So far, the passion of the island seemed to me mainly confined to things superficial or hysterical. This was not according to my guidebook.

"Well, not actually a revolution," said Trevor hastily. "More like a potential uprising. But still a major disturbance. Several years ago, Stanley tried to auction off the national art collection on the Internet. After it was discovered, most of the government ministers objected and the items were taken back. But there was much frank criticism and Stanley received many harsh letters of admonishment."

He added in a lower voice: "He has substantial debts from his bad investments. The entire affair was an embarrassment for him, as well as for the family."

"But wasn't there an outcry?" I asked. "Weren't people angry?"

"Of course," said Trevor resolutely. "There were the letters and many editorials, and while people don't talk about it, whenever you see him, it is always jiggling in the background, as they say. But he was allowed to continue. We are a forgiving nation. It is perhaps our best and worst quality."

"I don't understand," I said, mentally comparing Stanley's standing with Trevor's, whose best showing was far behind his brother's. "He's still ahead in all the polls."

Trevor looked at me fishily.

"I am aware that the current attention is with him," he said. "But that is due to the ability of most people to hear only the cacophony of government. They cannot appreciate sounds they are not used to hearing. But that is why you are here: to find and play the notes that will rouse them to their better instincts. With this, I am entrusting you."

———

The meeting lasted for another hour, and while I took notes copiously, at the end I remained unsure as to what they meant. As a reporter, I had been on the receiving end of this a few times; namely, an endless exercise in digression during which the list of questions is asked (repeatedly, sometimes) but nothing is gotten in return. Only fragments of responses and meandering half-thoughts that fissure out long before they evolve into any meaning. These types of interviews were always exhausting. In good faith, you did your homework, put in your time, and ended up merely being run around again and again. I'd since found the best thing to do in such situations was to end them yourself before you became overly resentful at being thrown into a useless pursuit. Which I was becoming and so which I did.

"I think I have enough to begin with," I finally said in the midst of a rare pause. By now, the subject matter had roamed from the spiritual nature of Momo-Jimans and the promise of greater cultural uplift, to more mundane matters such as forming strategic alliances with the other coconut and guava-producing nations in the region and administration of the island's mining rights. I did make one suggestion: to arrange a public disagreement with the Rector Froines on some trifling issue so that Trevor might appear more vigorous and forceful to voters—while at the same time taking advantage of the Rector's unpopularity—and to this tired campaign trick, he readily agreed.

There was no more mention of the revolution.

"I myself shall telephone the Rector," said Trevor as our conference drew to a close. "Despite his calling, he is appreciative of many of the responsbilities of secular life, particularly those involving politics."

He and the staff then stood and agreed it had been a productive first meeting. In particular, I noticed that Mr. Cecilia had produced a few dozen rolls of wrapped pennies and that Mrs. Murazami had rebraided the long cords holding her police whistle. But as they ushered me to the door (Trevor's limp now appearing on his right side), I had to turn my face away so they could not see my frozen look of distress. Increasingly, I had the feeling of being trapped inside an old sanitarium or a place like it, where the people were meaning to fundamentally change me in some way. Compounding this, I also felt the keen lack of anything in the way of personal resources. It was as if all my advantages, material and spiritual, had been stripped from me as they had been in jail. It was then that I thought of Wilkie, or more precisely, of Wilkie's car. If I could not have freedom of destiny, I thought, I could at least settle for personal mobility. Maybe having a car at my disposal would help me find something that I could use in my defense.

"As for my traveling, how would you suggest I get around?" I asked, putting a measure of hesitancy in my voice. "Should I rent a car or might Wilkie be able to drive me? I'm hardly accustomed to the roads here and I imagine I'll be traveling quite a bit in the next few weeks. I don't want to be a burden to the campaign."

Hearing the plebeian appeal, Trevor instantly stood himself up and looked at me imperiously. I knew that my overture had connected with his innermost vein of definition, that is, his fragile sense of importance. I also could see that much self-practicing had gone into his present gesture.

"Of course," he said, arching his fleshy brows in his best imitation of noblesse oblige. "You may have anything you wish. All you need to do is ask me each time."

VIII

AT THE HOTEL, I bade Wilkie good–bye and said I would phone for him later. I then shuffled up to my room where I dismissed my reporter's instinct to immediately reread and augment my notes and instead fetched the island's White Pages. Inside the thin book, I hunted down the home address and phone number of Stanley MacGower (listed as "S. and N. MacGower") and lay on the bed contemplating my next moves.

One matter was clear: given the nonsense of Trevor's ideas (not to mention how ludicrous he must look presenting them), there was no chance for success on his terms. Rather, the only promise lay in attacking the others'—particularly Stanley's—proposals and reforms. However, since Stanley's ideas likely lacked the ringing absurdities of his brother's, it also was true that a campaign of competing issues, even one in which Trevor's were mentioned in the deepest of relief, could not be waged and should be avoided at all costs.

This left the obvious: the dispiriting but invariably effective bludgeon of character assassination. The thought triggered in me an immediate distaste. As a reporter, I had covered my share of campaigns that had relied exclusively on such electioneering, with some of them completely devoid of any pretense that any issues should form the core of the public debate. I recalled one election ad that featured the grainy video of a man in a bathrobe shuffling down a street and then pitching forth into a heap as an empty whiskey bottle skittered away on the pavement. Over this gloomy night-time visage, the last name of the candidate's opponent then silently appeared in blood red. And in this case, not only did the senator who sponsored the commercial win the race, but he triumphed over the resulting libel suit as well.

Still, while mulling this over I realized with some comfort that my future need not be bound up in such efforts. Whether Trevor won or lost really was none of my concern. My only obligation was that he make a respectable showing, adequate enough to erase the charges pending against me. It was a miserable situation I was locked into but not a hopeless one. Bolstered by this, I grabbed a pen and began to attack my reporter's notebook, sifting for shards of ideas that might be cobbled together into a coherent theme or argument.

Fifteen minutes later, I heaved the pad aside, disgusted with myself for thinking there could be any redemption in the words I'd taken down. Since I had recorded everything faithfully, I now was able to view Trevor's unintelligible thinking in purely literal terms, unencumbered by the force of his personality. If anything, this made it worse since his rants brazenly displayed themselves. Now I truly saw no alternative. Any success that Trevor would achieve would have to come at the expense of his brother's failings, fabricated or not.

Reluctantly, I spread out a map of Momo-Jima on the bed and found Stanley's block in a suburb a few miles south of the capital, in a neighborhood called Nozomi-cho. I looked up the area in my guidebook but it was not mentioned. I paused, unsure of what I should do next. It was almost noon. Though my philosophy concerning all disagreeable tasks is to finish them as quickly as possible so I could better forget them (a habit that has often earned me praise for "having initiative"), my inertia, never far away when doing the unwanted bidding of others, was growing. Indeed, I had the distinct feeling that if I were to do what I really wanted—that is, lie down, close the curtains, and pull up the covers—I would not get up until the following afternoon, sleep for now being my only source of refuge. So struggling against this, I found Wilkie's number in my briefcase and asked him to meet me as soon as was convenient.

His battered Renault was idling in the same spot as before when I emerged from the hotel a half hour later. He let me open the back door for myself this time.

"Where to, Mr. Inoue?" Instead of glancing in his rearview mirror, Wilkie turned in his seat to look at me.

I hesitated before answering to perform a quick study on his face. Was there some genuine earnestness in his expression? Some natural sympathy for human circumstance? Whatever it was, I had to make an instant decision. I was about to take him partly into my confidence, and in doing so, I would know immediately if my assessment of him was correct.

"I'd like to go to Nozomi-cho," I said casually. "On Omo-dori. The number is 945."

Whether he knew the address or not, he didn't let on. I let it hang for a moment, then added, "To Stanley MacGower's house."

A benign surprise played across Wilkie's peaceable face, a look that he restrained as much as he could. Still, in his reaction I detected what I thought was the hint of an immanent rapport.

"I didn't know he'd moved back there," was his only comment before turning around to drive.

—

We arrived at the house in under ten minutes. It was located in an old residential area that was middle-class at the edges but poorer the deeper inside you ventured, with several of the interior blocks filled with low, single-story apartments that resembled Spanish-style compounds. Stanley's house was large and neatly kept and distinguished by an old Oldsmobile moored up on blocks on the front lawn and a backward-leaning chain-link fence that surrounded the lot. Despite this, in contrast to Trevor's, the house took its place plainly, as just another home in the neighborhood, with none of the election signs or stickers that had identified his brother's. The salary for elected leaders here must be grim, I thought, surveying it.

"Do you want me to wait or come back?" asked Wilkie. Betraying no overt curiosity over his mission, he again turned in his seat to address me.

"Wait, please," I said. Now that we had arrived, I had become palpably nervous over what I'd planned to do, suddenly aware that it is one thing to dream up an enterprise and another to picture yourself carrying it out. Casually, I took one of my new ballpoints from my pocket and clicked it open and closed repeatedly as if lost in thought. I noticed Wilkie was looking at me closely. Perhaps I could begin my appeal to him now, I thought.

"How did you come to work for Trevor?" I asked as unconcernedly as I could.

"Oh, I don't work for him directly," Wilkie responded. "I work for the family, for Grandmama's estate. She hired me as her driver years ago. It's only when Mr. MacGower said he needed someone that her lawyers sent me."

"When was that?"

"About three months ago. Not so long."

"And how do you like working for Trevor?"

"We-ell." He drew out the word, a little unsure of my intent and his moon face registered a queerness over my inquiry. "It's all right. He's no trouble most of the time. I used to work at a hospital in pick up and delivery. You should see how the doctors there treat their staff. They don't know the first thing about people." He stopped. "Why do you want to know?"

"Just curious. This is my first day working for him. I'd like to get a sense of how it might turn out."

"You'll probably find out a lot more about him than I have. I just drive him around. But I can tell you, he can get angry sometimes if things don't go his way. I remember once he threw a frozen meat pie at Mr. Cecilia for buying the wrong kind of sign paint. But his aim was bad and he ended-up just busting one of his TVs."

"I see," I said slowly, as if this were a revelation I was absorbing. "That was just the one time, though?"

He nodded. "Just the once."

"Let me ask you . . ." (I dropped my voice now to give it a conspiratorial edge.) "What do you suppose are his chances of winning?"

Wilkie thought before answering.

"Probably not too good, but I can't truly say. I don't concern myself too much with politics. It goes in one ear and then I forget it. My real last name is Bamberpays. Mr. MacGower said he wanted to call me Wilkie after one of his favorite political leaders."

"But in the last few months, I'm sure you've gotten to know him. Have you thought how he might be as president?"

"I suppose," he said unconvincingly. "But from what most people say, I don't think he's going to win."

"That's what I've heard, too."

I sighed and settled back in my seat, as if ruefully acknowledging the inevitability of difficult circumstances. I looked out to Stanley's house. The neighborhood seemed extraordinarily quiet in the bright midday sun. There was not a sound coming from anywhere except for the mice-like chattering of birds and the overhead whine of a far-off plane.

"Are you wondering why we're here?" I asked after a moment.

"Well, sort of." He stopped as if he'd said the wrong thing.

"Go on."

"But this is the kind of work you do, isn't it? I mean, Mr. Mac-Gower's never had a manager before. He's had advisors but he's always gone his own way."

"I'm not really his manager, more like a coordinator. But you're right. This is the sort of thing we do. We figure out the people we're working for and then we figure out the people we're running against. First you realize your own strengths, then you identify the other person's weaknesses."

"So you're here to understand Mr. MacGower's brother."

"More than that," I said, putting a note of urgency in my voice. "I want to know everything about him. How he feels, how he thinks, and how he thinks he's going to win. To know him as well as he knows himself. People are usually their own source of trouble."

Some of the gravity with which I said this must have affected Wilkie who was now still, not moving a twitch, his mouth slightly

open. But that was not the look I'd hoped for. What I was appealing for was the look of an intuitive man being drawn into a confidence. I waited but it failed to materialize.

"I'm going to need your help," I said finally. "We're already well
behind and there's thousands of things that need to be done. I can't
afford to squander any chances."

"Well, of course, you've got it," said Wilkie instantly, feeling
now that he'd grasped the innuendo. "Just because I don't follow
politics doesn't mean I don't want Mr. MacGower to win. I like
him. He . . ."—and here Wilkie nodded toward Stanley's home—
"hasn't ever spoken to me, ever. Even to ask a favor. And I've been
around him plenty of times. Mr. MacGower's never done that."

His voice now took on the conspiratorial tone.

"What would you like me to do?"

Such quick acquiescence should have comforted me but instead
Wilkie's eagerness and open-mindedness made me feel more alone
than ever. If I were to ask for help, I thought, I probably would have
to provide the sort of explicit instructions that I precisely didn't
want to think about. As such, Wilkie would be less an ally than an
eager subordinate, capable mainly of being managed. Or in short, I
was on my own again, responsible for my own way through things.

"Nothing," I said emptily, then hastened, "for now."

I looked back to the house, steeling myself for the next encounter and trying to rid myself of any fear, hope or expectation. I
opened the car door and stepped out.

"Are you sure you don't mind waiting?" I asked.

"Of course not," said Wilkie, cheered now that he had been tak-
en into my confidence and perhaps sensing himself as a full accom-
plice in my machinations. He turned on the car stereo to a loud
burst of mournful music. "Take as long as you need but to tell the
truth, I don't think he's all that complicated. I'm sure you'll have
him figured out soon enough. "

IX

Walking cheerlessly up the cracked concrete path to Stanley's house, I stopped to examine the blocked Oldsmobile. Despite the fitful tropical weather, the old car was in good shape and seemed to have been consistently cared for. The paint was of a good brownish ebony, the off-white interior was whole and unblemished, and the undercarriage looked to be free of rust. All of the sloped chrome and grillwork was intact as well. Except for the missing tires, the car appeared quite serviceable, maybe even valuable, a quality that was heightened by its overall oddity in this time and place.

As I stood admiring it, a woman's voice addressed me from behind. It was a timorous call, more like that of a small animal than a person.

"Have you come about the car?"

"I'm looking for Mr. MacGower," I said, turning and shading the full sun with my hand. Through my fingers, I managed to make out a thin woman in a print dress with large, overblown hair and an almost terrified countenance about her.

"Who are you?"

"Benjamin Inoue."

"Oh, the man Trevor hired."

She said this with no sense of accusation or injury, as I would have expected from someone in the opposition camp. Instead, there was almost a sense of relief in her voice and perhaps even a relaxation in her anxious pose. Disarmed at her reaction, as well at her knowing who I was, I suddenly felt awkward, as if I were a guest arriving late to a function in my honor.

"Please come in," she said. "I'll get him. I'm Mrs. MacGower."

She turned and I followed her into the house. Her gait, like her manner, had a tense and hurried quality to it and again the picture of a small woodland creature came to mind. Hastily she opened the door for me, told me to be comfortable in the disordered living room, and then disappeared out a back door like a match that had been blown out. From where I stood, I could hear the fading of her clattering footsteps and the noises and thumping of several children upstairs at play, a gang thick in the spirit of combative fun. After a few moments, I then heard the heavier pounding of purposeful men's feet.

As he strode into the room, however, Stanley MacGower appeared even more distressed-looking than his wife. Equally as thin, he was narrow-chested with curiously underdeveloped upper arms and shoulders, as if he had scrupulously avoided any sort of physical exertion throughout his life. Owing perhaps to his anxiety, his hair was sparse and prematurely gray and his skin, like his brother's, was almost unnaturally pale. I guessed him to be in his early fifties, though he looked older. When he offered his hand, the big bony knobs at his elbows stuck out at odd angles to his body.

"Stanley MacGower," he said. "This is a coincidence. I was about to call you."

Shaking his fleshless hand, it struck me that Trevor's brother was as unlikely a high-ranking government official as I've met. Nothing in his presence radiated the slightest aura of power, or of even having a reluctant ambition for it, and it seemed the hand I now held would have belonged more appropriately to a breeder of pet fish or a druggist's assistant. Moreover, it also occurred to me that I had seen no evidence so far of Stanley's political career. Not one sign, button, or framed photograph attesting to his public ambitions or office. All over the island I saw his red and white campaign boards stuck to buses and trees and in storefronts but in his home, nothing.

"Benjamin Inoue."

"Yes, of course. Does Trevor know you're here?"

It was an abrupt question, asked hurriedly under his breath. But as is the case when assaulted with a sudden and personal inquiry, the human instinct to give an undeserved but truthful answer took over.

"No, I came on my own."

"This is fortunate," said Stanley, who turned to his wife. "Nao, chase the children from upstairs. I want to meet with Ben in the study."

While she ran up, Stanley took my arm.

"I heard you're American."

"That's right."

"Born and raised?"

"Yes."

"Then perhaps you'll know how to handle this. I was about to start searching for your telephone number when you appeared. It really is a stroke."

He smiled enigmatically and began leading me to the stairs. That I had no idea what he was referring to, or that he even stopped to explain himself, made it seem natural for me to be led through his cluttered home. Then I realized, of course, that this self-involved quality of Stanley's was Trevor's as well.

As we reached the staircase, several obedient children, along with Nao clutching a sleeping infant, appeared at the top step. They fell silent when they caught sight of me.

"Come on, come on," said Stanley irritably to them. "We have a guest."

Reluctantly, they began clumping down the stairs. As they did, a petite young woman with longish black hair and a simple turquoise dress appeared behind them. Too old to be part of the group, she also didn't seem associated with the family, either; I guessed her to be a close friend or neighbor. But as the children assembled around me at the foot of the stairs, she remained at the top, seemingly indecisive over whether I merited coming down to greet. Or was it that she was taking the chance to fully examine me? For I got that feeling, too.

"Here are the children, every bloody one of them," said Stanley with only the faintest measure of humor. "This is Oliver and Ophelia and Charles and Chloe." He waved his hand over them but did not stop to distinguish their identities. "And Nao's got Harlan, who's twelve weeks today."

The rest of the children appeared to be between four and eight with the two boys the oldest. As they forced out their greetings, the dark-haired woman slowly began to descend the staircase, moving with careful discernment as if testing each step to see if it would hold her weight. The effect naturally heightened her presence throughout the room.

"And this is Nao's sister, Sono. She's been helping us since Nao came down with the milk fever. Or so she says it's fever."

Still clutching the railing, Sono extended her hand. As I grasped it, I felt a cool, dry touch. She let out a brief murmur of address and stepped back.

I also murmured a small greeting and used the opportunity to more frankly assess her. In addition to the very black hair that hung to her shoulders, she had large oval eyes and higher-than-typical cheekbones. Her skin was a yellowish-olive, darker than her sister's, and she was smaller in height—barely five-foot now that I saw her on level ground. The loose turquoise dress went well with her coloring, and her straw-colored sandals with their small heels accentuated the slight curve of her lower calves and ankles.

I must have lingered in my appraisal for I felt Stanley's fingers suddenly tighten around my forearm.

"Is the study clear?" he demanded of his wife and children, giving me a slight shove forward. "Picked up all of your things and toys?"

"Nothing's underfoot," said his wife rocking the baby, who was struggling in infant communication.

"Then we're not to be disturbed. Leave us alone until we come down." Stanley was already taking the first steps up the stairs and his pushing of me now became insistent pulling. I stole one more look at Sono (her eyes now turned away from me) as I found myself being dragged onto the steps.

"I'll send up plates for lunch."

"No interruptions," he glared.

Rapidly we then ascended the stairs, Stanley not letting go of my arm until we entered the study and he'd pushed me into a stiff wooden-backed chair in the middle of the room. Contrary to his wife's assertion, though, I saw the study hardly had been cleared of debris. Scattered around us were the remains of a toy train set, bowls of half-eaten cereal, many open video boxes, and out of the corner of my eye, a small, fast-moving pet. Perhaps this was what "picked up" meant when you had children, I thought. Once again, I was conscious of the utter lack of political trappings.

"First, you must understand one thing," said Stanley, who'd gotten a small desk chair and pushed it so that he was mere inches from me. "I am not crazy and you must not treat me as if I am." He spoke with great deliberateness and I could smell the meat and garlic of his lunch on his breath. There also was the film of a drink or two in his eyes.

"I had no intention of that," I said with surprise, both at his words and his sudden assault on me. "Why would you think...?"

"It's the natural conclusion of anyone who knows my brother," he interrupted. "I wouldn't fully trust anyone who thought otherwise, or who would want to know me based on their dealings with him. Usually, I have to spend a good half hour or so convincing people of my credibility if they've met him before me. Tell me, what do you find to be his most ridiculous characteristic?"

His words came at me like a hard funnel of water, intended to saturate the listener, not communicate with him. In this way, too, I thought, he was very much like his brother. I paused, searching for an appropriate response.

"Never mind. I know it's difficult to choose among them. Even I, knowing him since childhood, have never resolved this completely. Care for a drink?"

I nodded, more from reflex than desire.

"Good. We can start to trust each other." He turned around and snatched up a bottle from the floor and poured much of it into two child's plastic tumblers. Watching Stanley, it seemed as if he were constantly being reminded of things he needed to attend to. He took a generous swallow and addressed me.

"Let me say that I also despise the belief in coincidence, so to me your being here is a fortuitous event, nothing more. As I mentioned, I was about to call you. It is not for me to begin a new belief system so late in life."

"Why were you going to call me?"

"I also heard how Trevor hired you," he replied, not answering me. "In jail and facing charges. But this is not to cast aspersions. My brother, despite his many character flaws, is a good assessor of abilities. It's the Cartesian nature he inherited from our French governors. He thinks himself equal to his superiors and superior to his equals."

"Why were you going to call me?" I asked again.

Stanley poured himself the remainder of the bottle. He relaxed and leaned back in his chair, regarding me as if I were a friendly adversary out to cheat him.

"Has Trevor mentioned to you our late grandmother, Regina Angela? I'm sure he has, in one way or another. She's the one responsible for all of us. She was the last of the Wimpleburtons, one of the first British families on this island. 'The Wimpleburtons were here before the first buildings were built,' she used to say. Here, this might help."

Striding to a bookcase, he pulled down a large gilt-edged book similar to a school annual and handed it to me. Opening it, I saw it was a thick album of old family history filled with faded photographs, engraved invitations to public events, and many newspaper articles cut from the society section. From the dates, I guessed its chronology began about two generations ago and continued to the near-present, though the number of recent entries was comparatively fewer. As I leafed through it, I recognized several photos of Trevor, including one of him as a young man standing pensively on the prow of a yacht and looking at a large gathering of people on shore. I closed it and saw embossed on its spine the letters "RAW."

"Very impressive," I said neutrally.

"Yes, Grandmama and her family were quite a presence, though God forbid my saying, she is also the root of my problem."

"Why is that?"

"Her traditions," he said. "Because she was the last of the line, Grandmama was deeply attached to them. The Wimpleburtons have always enjoyed their influence on the island, not to mention the family legacy. Grandmama was committed to seeing that our position did not perish."

Stanley took the album back from me.

"And that is where you can help me," he said.

I suddenly didn't like where I was being led to in this exchange, nor the noticeable change in tone in Stanley's voice. Or perhaps it was simply the allusion to money, which debases most human conversation and which had often done so with me.

"How?" I asked, taking a wary sip of my drink.

This time I saw a slight hesitation—or was it something else?—from Stanley before he continued.

"This is extremely private, but of course, I have no choice," he said, replacing the annual in the bookcase. "I only burden you with this so that you may know the full extent of my dilemma." He remained standing and began to address me.

"For years, my brother and I have been supported by Grandmama's estate," he said. "It is not an excessive amount of money, given that the family wealth has been depleted by unfortunate investments, but it always has been more than sufficient, even with my present wife and children. In fact, I have been much surprised by her largesse in death, given that when she was alive, Grandmama was considerably less generous. Still, though, her legacy has always depended on one provision: that either Trevor or I continue to occupy one of the presidential offices. She had no preference as to whom, her only desire was that a Wimpleburton be represented in the higher realms of power. But because of this, to maintain our inheritance, one of us must always remain as president or vice president."

I felt I now sensed what he was driving at and that he was about to make his forthright appeal. I spoke brusquely to cut him off.

"You can't expect me to go behind Trevor to help you," I exclaimed. "I've never heard of such a thing. Are you that worried about your brother? Is he that much of a threat?" I then added self-righteously, "Are you that much in debt?"

Stanley fixed me with a pitying look.

"Of course I'm not worried," he said evenly. "I know my brother better than anyone. I've known his true nature since we were children. Do you think I'm deranged as he? I know he cannot win. What I want from you is the opposite."

"The opposite?" My sense of affront faltered and I searched Stanley's unperturbed face for clarification.

"I don't understand," I said finally.

"Let me explain my position to you."

Stanley again seated himself next to me and his errant mouth began twitching once more with explanation.

"The book you just examined is nearly a complete history of the family for the last seventy-five years, though there are other, equally tiresome books here, as well," he said. "In any of them, you can chart the course of our more recent presence on Momo-Jima. There are Wimpleburton weddings, Wimpleburton parties, Wimpleburton comings-out, even an annual Wimpleburton ball that used to take place for the benefit of the native foods society. We are a well-documented clan." His eyes glittered. "But there is one thing you won't find in them. In that book, did you happen to notice any photographs of me as a young man?"

Now that he'd mentioned it, I was suddenly aware of his conspicuous absence. He smiled a bit evilly at my chagrin.

"I am missing from everything from my early twenties until the time I was nearly forty. About fifteen years, overall, though it seemed much shorter when I was living it. And it feels even shorter than that now. Do you know where I was?

I shook my head.

"I was out exploring the world, every damned bit of it, because I knew one day I would have to come back to this rotten little blip of a place and take up my role in things," he said savagely. "My expected duties, even if no one could tell me what was expected. Duties that I have been performing for more than a decade and even still I don't have any better idea of what they are."

He went on, delving deeper into his rage and spurred on by my bewilderment.

"Surprised? I don't think you should be. You've spent barely a week here. Imagine spending the first twenty years of your life, and then after that, the sentence to stay. You'd have been long out of your mind. It's not what it seems from the outside. Location is the stupidest of destinies!"

As he punctuated his remarks, the child's tumbler flew out of his hand. Angrily, he regained it, filled it again, and drank, calming himself.

"What I was getting at was that I got the chance to see things, move around the world and see where I might fit in," he said more steadily. "And it was then I decided that one day, I would leave this place permanently. Leave it to those who value its homely traits. Leave it forever when I could."

As he spoke, I felt a shock break over me. Now I simply sat, looking at a large map of the island that was hung up over his desk and which had been heavily defaced with crayon scrawls.

"If that's the case, why not just leave?" I asked in a low voice. "Let Trevor become president."

As soon as the words left my mouth, I regretted them.

"Leave? How can I?" Stanley's vehemence again sprang forth, this time, it seemed, from a sense of personal injury. "He's finished completely last both times he's run. In the past, he's proposed building monorails to the nearest islands, establishing a national dress code, and dragging icebergs from the polar icecaps to make bottled water for export. On his best behavior, he's a presentable lunatic. He can't be victorious so I must be . . . always, I must be."

Like the opening iris of a camera lens, the bigger light emerged for me, even as I was aware that the illumination came from only a slightly more credible source.

"You want me to see that Trevor wins," I said, astonished. "So that you can lose."

Stanley's face was grim. He tried to force a smile onto his face but only the blunt rictus of his mouth emerged.

"I've spent years trying to raise the money to live elsewhere but this really is the best solution, isn't it? I've already planned the departure. The morning after the election, we'll leave for somewhere, anywhere, and forward the estate checks. There's even a place in Scotland, Grimspew, where the Wimpleburtons have been since the time of dust or so. I've heard I can arrange an earldom if I become a citizen and pay off some back taxes. I'll even have a government pension due me. No one will be the wiser."

"But Trevor is a buffoon, you just said so. How could he run a country? And how could you leave him in charge? This is your home, even if you despise it."

"It's you, not me, who's working for him," said Stanley icily. "Besides, you're assuming there are things here to govern, things to preserve. But this island always has run itself and there is precious little left to ruin. Whatever was put in place long ago still exists, despite all the attempts to change things. It's a very old mentality and that's the way it will always be. Can't you see why Grandmama was wedded?"

What he was saying was true. During my brief tourist appraisal, I had seen the country display its present-day shabbiness at every turn, and do so without any degree of self-consciousness; it was the manner of old gentility that doesn't care to know the towels have grown thin, the servants have left, and the furnishings are past rescue. This was a part of the world that still ran on gas and wires, and on telephones and telegrams, and on the post and hard currencies, with no information from the newer parts of the century.

And the question was: Did I like these sorts of conditions or not? I wondered briefly then turned back to the present matter.

"All of what you're saying may be true," I began, "but it doesn't help your brother. He's not going to win. He'll still finish dead last. You may lose but so what?"

"Most of the others are no threat. They're only being supported because people are confused. Really, only Van Gland stands an outside chance. If we wish to make it so, it'll be just me and him."

"We?"

His expression became sharper.

"How much is Trevor paying you?"

"I can't tell you that."

"Doesn't matter, I'll double it. Or just keep your job with him, it's easier that way."

"Are you suggesting . . . ?"

"It makes the most natural sense. It's the perfect opportunity."

"I can't work for both of you. It's unethical."

"It's what everyone wants."

"What about Trevor? He'll find out."

"You'll see that he doesn't."

"It's ridiculous. There must be a law against it."

"There used to be. I—we'll change it."

"There must be another way."

"There isn't. And don't forget, I am yet the vice president, with full powers of office. And you are here only as a tourist, and one who's been charged with several counts of fraud at that. I know you have your objections but I would be careful about raising them too strongly. There are other factors at stake."

Abruptly, Stanley then waved his thin hand and his countenance relaxed, even as my agitation now swelled. There was the unseen part of my character that he (like Trevor) had located and capitalized on, and like all skillful victors, he was prepared to take his triumph benignly so as not to equate my plane of emotions with what he was feeling. Still, for many minutes, I gamely made a case for my freedom, even as I recognized my gestures for what they were. For again, as with Trevor, there was a certain element in Stanley that was unreachable, not merely self-occupied, and in the end he did not dismiss me from his consideration as much as remove me from his consciousness.

"Don't think of it as ill-principled, Ben," he said after my objections had run their course and I sat before him beleaguered, despairing, and finally, speechless. "Think of it as a way to bring justice to everyone concerned. For Trevor, Grandmama, and of course, for myself."

X

LATER IN RECALLING my first meeting with Stanley, it surprised me that I didn't stop then to fully consider all the implications of he and Trevor being brothers (especially since I'd been with the other only hours earlier), and that in the end, they were likely to possess more, and more complicated, inward similarities than outward differences. I don't know whether the latter course of things would have been easier or substantially different, but certainly my thoughts on matters would have changed, and given that one's thoughts provide the only real source of solace, that is of no small concern.

As I remember it, I rushed to leave Stanley's house ("bolted" is the more apt word), pausing only to stutter a curt good-bye to Stanley's wife and nearly turn an ankle stepping into an upturned child's bicycle helmet. I did have enough presence of mind to look for Sono but she was nowhere in sight.

When I got outside, Wilkie also was nowhere to be seen and for a moment I thought he had misunderstood me and that I'd have to wait for him to return (thinking also that I would rather linger on the street than re-enter that deluded, torn-apart household). But then I saw his Renault parked down the block under a cluster of kapok trees and heard the sounds of opera blaring from his car speakers.

When he saw me approaching, he partially turned down the music and swung open the back door.

"Did you get what you wanted?" he asked. He was even more cheerful than when I'd left him. The distressing music had put him in a good mood.

"Sort of," I muttered, awash in the scalding bath of self-ridicule. When Wilkie saw me last, I was stepping forward with, if not determination and expectancy, at least a modicum of purpose. Now even that had been drained from me and replaced with an abject humiliation. I took off my coat and got heavily into the car.

"What is that?" I asked.

"Ponchielli, *La Gioconda*," he said with pleasure. "Beautiful and grand."

So that he didn't get the notion to turn it up again (normally I am fine with such matters, but not now), I quickly unhatched my briefcase, took out some papers, and pretended to study them. As Wilkie waited, I saw his eyes become half-lidded and his knuckles begin to keep *allegretto* on the steering wheel. One should never attempt to question the source of another man's passion, I thought. It can only underestimate the both of you.

I let a few moments of purposeless shuffling go by, feeling more dispirited with every aria and recitative. Looking though my materials, I suddenly was struck by how much information I now was responsible for . . . and how little of it made sense. I also saw that one of my cheap new markers had leaked and ruined the file Trevor had prepared for me on "FAVORITE DOMESTIC ANIMALS." I shut my briefcase and laid it on the seat, not wishing to acknowledge any of its contents.

"So what's your impression of Stanley?" I asked Wilkie for the lack of anything better to say.

"You mean, what kind of person do I think he is?" he answered, his eyes opening with a draggy reluctance.

I nodded.

"Nothing special," said Wilkie, thinking. "Just an unhappy man with a wife and kids, isn't that usually it? Like I said, he's never spoken to me. More than ten years, too."

"What about Nao?"

"If that's his wife now, I never met her."

"He was married before?"

"Once, a long time ago. I never met her either, but I saw pictures."

"Do you remember anything about her?"

Wilkie considered. "She had a face kind of like a ferret's, only not so many whiskers."

I sighed. "What about the grandmother? Do you remember what she used to say about him?"

"Some." His eyes were open now. "She didn't talk too much about the family. She would only say something at the start of the month when she was writing the checks."

He stopped with the employee's instinct not to talk too freely about his employer.

"It's all right," I said, "I know how they live. What did she say?"

He hesitated.

"It was usually something about Trevor. How he should either get married or go back to radio school. That's what he was studying a long time ago, radio engineering. Honestly, I think that when she thought of him, he annoyed her."

That certainly rang true, I reflected.

"Anything else? What was she like?"

Wilkie shook his head. I thought I saw a flicker of old loyalty pass through his thoughts.

"She didn't get involved much with the relatives who were living. What she liked best was the past. When I was working there, I got paid mostly to do her files. She was a funny woman. Some days she'd wouldn't talk to you, other times she'd make me lunch, give me tickets to a movie or a concert and let me have the day off. But overall, usually nice."

He snapped off the opera and started the car, seemingly to close off my questioning.

"So, where to?" he asked.

I grumbled something low and incomprehensible, distracted from deep inside. It was occurring to me that with every question I asked, I was accumulating more and more unwanted knowledge—knowledge I would then have to store, categorize, and bring forth when necessary. Yet to free myself of my predicament, a stretch of even more disagreeable stockpiling was required. In effect, my final freedom would require an initial period of greater enslavement. I wondered where the Maginot Line of data absorption might be; at what point would I be able to push past these concerns and be allowed to think my own unrestrained thoughts? It seemed a long way off.

This was not a good state for me, I knew. As unpleasant as the jail experience had been, the kinds of mental traps I was now experiencing were more dangerous because they threatened to turn my thinking beyond reason. I suddenly fantasized about commandeering Wilkie and staging a late run to the airport, or heading out to the harbor and finding refuge in the stinking hold of an outbound freighter. But then I realized that even these desperate scenarios were sunk in futility: the island was serviced by only two flights a week (the next one due in three days) and at present, there were no ships in port because despite Trevor's pronouncements, there were embarrassingly few exports to speak of. Only the sapodilla, an occasional boatload of green, undersized coconuts, and then the giant granadilla, and the latter only in high summer, which was roughly two months from now.

"I suppose I should be getting back," I said, looking up to Stanley's house to perhaps get another glimpse of Sono, or perhaps a clue into my next, most immediate destiny. But the lawn was empty and there was no movement at the windows—no running children, no presidential candidates, candidate's wives, or sisters-in-law. There was only the old, faithful Oldsmobile, waiting in the burning sun for someone to come along and rescue it. Just like me, I concluded unhappily.

XI

When I called Trevor to apprise him of my meeting with Stanley (for in returning home with Wilkie I felt duty-bound to at least mention that I'd met his brother), he was pleased.

"A master move," he said sagely. "Keep the enemy off balance. Unorthodox tactics. The secret to any successful sortie."

He didn't bother to inquire why I had chosen to go to Stanley's or what we had talked about, nor did I elaborate on either. Instead, he used my presence to run through the docket of his most recent thoughts, including that day's press coverage, the fluctuations in interest rates at the national bank, and the upcoming weather patterns to election day. Despite their common gloomy outlook, especially the newspaper coverage, he exuded optimism.

"I'm going to have to call off our meeting tonight," he said abruptly at the end of our conversation, his voice blasting through the phone receiver that I had become accustomed to holding several inches from my ear. "Minor health disturbance. Nothing to be troubled about. I'll send Wilkie around for you tomorrow at eight. Can't wait to see what you've cooked up."

Per usual, he banged down the phone without warning. I was now left with the sense of immediate relief, as well as the dwindling remainder of the afternoon. In a long moment of debate, I again considered filling a knapsack with beer and a blanket and taking myself out of the silly president-making business to sleep and dream on the sticky pink sand for a few hours. But as before, I knew that if I were to divert my attention to other things, even if for a short time, I would not address my work at all that day. This matter at hand was much like taking apart an unfamiliar piece of machinery; the more you disassembled, the more responsibility you accrued for finishing the overall task.

On an impulse, and for the added need to be held to my duties, I phoned Stanley. It occurred to me that I had left his house with no clear understanding of what was required of me, other than that I was being employed to fix the results of a democratic presidential election. Now I wanted to clarify matters before too much might be expected of me, as well as get some instructive words from the slightly more coherent brother. But the phone rang for upwards of a minute—I allowed for the squalor of five children to drown it out—and no one responded. He was probably out pricing royal titles, I thought bitterly, or lining up the sale of his home and the purchase of a new one.

With no better alternative in sight, I then went to the lobby to pilfer the day's newspapers. Making off with copies of each daily (as well as several of the pastries and chocolate cookies that had been put out for afternoon tea), I took them up to my room and went through them at length, though surprisingly they contained little election coverage. While I again noted that the *Morning Gleaner* was disagreeable toward Trevor and the *News Review* was charitably ignorant, most of the pages today were given over to accident photos, real estate ads, and optimistic religious canards. Then I remembered that yesterday was Sunday and that the slow tide of things here was probably drifting even more tediously than usual.

However, it was while reading the brief *Morning Gleaner* story ("CANDIDATES SUPPORT POULTRY CRACKDOWN"), that I suddenly wondered if I shouldn't phone up the reporter (again R. S. Bando) and introduce myself to head off any further negative reporting. Though as a journalist, I'd always despised those who operated this way, it seemed that as a campaign advisor this was precisely the sort of rank work I should be engaged in. Mulling this over, I felt another of my principles of professional behavior slipping away.

I was scanning the newspaper for its telephone number when simultaneously the phone buzzed and a heavy knocking erupted at the door. I picked up the phone first and heard the low tones of the desk clerk who'd reported me to the police, and whom I now assumed was calling about the stolen croissants.

"You have a visitor on his way up," he said with his customary rancor. "In the future, please tell the desk of all arrivals." Not wishing to listen any further, I banged down the phone in the manner I'd learned from Trevor and went to the door.

Waiting for me in the hallway was the fattest man I have ever met. In his mid-sixties, he wore a cream and gold pin-striped suit, along with a white shirt and old-fashioned greenshade sunglasses that were pressed tightly into the fleshy sides of his face. I guessed his weight at easily more than four hundred pounds, though his height was roughly equal to mine. His tie, shoes, and socks also were cream and wisps of fine old hair curled down from the apex of his head to wrap around his ears.

"Mr. Inoue?"

I nodded.

"May I come in? I'm a friend of Trevor's. I'm afraid it's crucial to your work."

He appeared so diffident in spite of his physical bulk that after a brief hesitation, I stood aside to let him enter and indicated the room's lone desk chair, or bed, for him to sit on. Taking off his sunglasses, the man then turned sideways through the door and headed directly for the bed. As he sat on it, he sank so deeply into the mattress, even creasing the boxspring, that I feared he would not be able to get up. In the confines of the small room, and with his light-colored clothing, he reminded me of an enormous marshmallow.

"My name is Rector Arthur Froines," he said. "Might I have some water? It's extremely severe outside."

Taken aback, I nevertheless hurried straight to the bathroom (urged on by the thought that he might be in some sort of physical distress), drew sink water into a plastic cup and gave it to him. He drank the contents in one steady swallow and then spoke pleasantly.

"I'm very glad to know that Trevor has put a professional in charge of things," he said. "I understand he's given you my name for use in his campaign." His voice, emanating from the deep well of a fat man's body, sounded surprisingly reedy and clipped.

"He wanted to arrange a disagreement with you," I said. "A staged one, I'm afraid."

"The fruit export issue, of course," he said, nodding. "Tell him I'll be happy to argue with him and give it a good public show. Please call my assistant Mr. Brunt and tell him when Trevor needs me." With difficulty, he reached into his jacket, pulled out a card and gave it to me. On it was printed just his name and a phone number.

"Thank you. I'm sure it will be extremely helpful."

"Not at all. Trevor and I have recently found ourselves fully aligned on our political opinions and I am always willing to aid a worthy candidate. It is my duty as a Momo-Jiman, and my responsibility as a guardian of the human spirit. I take both very seriously. However, what I came about today is a different matter. Did Trevor tell you of my current position?"

"He said you represent the growers here."

"Yes, that's it. President of the Greater Momo-Jiman Land and Fruit League, though vegetables are our concern as well. Four hundred and twelve members and over one half million square acres. Now is our sixty-first year and we are the eighteenth largest produce league in the Oceanic region. Still, it's an impossible position that gets more difficult every year. I have to wear several hats, as you Americans say. Land use covers a range of concerns."

"It sounds extremely broad."

"And this is in addition to my religious duties, which I tend to daily at my church," he said. "That, of course, is still my highest priority. Blessed are the true fanatics."

"Of course."

Rector Froines beamed at me and went on.

"Nevertheless, I am proud to be influencing such an important matter for our country. It is land that gives us our sustenance and our future, both of which we must zealously guard. For example, one of my responsibilities is mining, which is a particularly difficult issue here. Did you know that digging for minerals is illegal in all of Momo-Jima? Or that since our moratorium on gemstone mining, there has not been a pit dug deeper than twelve feet anywhere on the island? When one of our most famous cricketeers died and we wanted to excavate a commemorative resting place for him, we had to get a law passed. That was Georges Li."

"I didn't know he was Momo-Jiman," I lied, having never before heard of him.

Rector Froines nodded. "As head of the land union, such matters regularly come before me because of our delicate balance between the agrarian and the industrial. Today, to obtain a permit to drill or mine in Momo-Jima is practically impossible. To some, this fact symbolizes our country's rediscovered pride in our most valued commodity—the landscape around us. Yet to others, this signifies our adherence to an archaic notion that leaves us a nation undecided if we endorse the past or present."

"It's fortunate then that you have this election," I replied non-committedly. "It could be an avenue for progress."

"Perhaps," said Rector Froines, equally ambiguous. "Still, it is mostly a non-issue. All the candidates long ago have decided to support the extension of our mining embargo. That is, all except for Trevor, who has called for its repeal. It's part of his 'Greater Momo-Jimans For Greater Momo-Jima' initiative. Truly, it's the one issue on which we disagree. And I'm forced to admit, there has been a noticeable response to his stance. Some people even have begun to support him because of it." The rector looked at me directly and I noticed that his easy smile had disappeared and that a hard feeling had forced its way onto his large potato face.

"And that is the root of my problem," he said.

It was the second time that afternoon I had heard and felt a threat from that phrase but still not understood it. I also felt a stab of dread as I realized how prominently I was now figuring into so many others' thinking.

"What is the root?" I asked blandly.

"Trevor means well, naturally," continued Rector Froines. "But sometimes he can be blind to the more urgent realities around him.

One reality is that we are a developing nation and must be treated as such."

With that, Rector Froines held out his plastic cup in mute request for more water. Again, I hurried to the bathroom to fill it. And again, I waited in silence until he finished drinking and continued to speak.

"What I mean to say is that we are not like First World countries such as yours," he went on. "We function differently. It is not a question of scale but of nature. Of course we are desirous of progress, but such development proceeds much more uniquely with us. That is the fundamental nature of governance here."

There was little use trying to conceal my confusion over his words and motivations. Perhaps because I was overtired and overwhelmed with so much recent information, I could not translate what he was saying into any logical statement of purpose. His words to me seemed both familiar and unreachable. And not only that, I thought, but if I somehow were to understand what he was saying, here was yet another unseen angle to things. I sat down at the small desk, oppressed with the prospect of more new knowledge to absorb and interpret.

Rector Froines smiled sympathetically at me.

"All right, Mr. Inoue, brass tacks, as you say. We at the league have a very deep interest in preserving the traditions of Momo-Jima. For myself, the old ways have survived not only because we venerate them, but because they assure us the most quality and profitability. And in our opinion, Trevor's proposal to reverse our long-held mining tradition will be a great hindrance to our developing economy."

"But how [and here I could hear several forlorn notes edging into my voice] will preventing development help your country?"

"This is what I mean," said the rector emphatically. "This is not like your nation where the markets operate smoothly along established precedents. In countries such as ours, the markets are still young and being forged. For us, the more flexible methods work best. Perhaps you would call our markets more informal and adaptable, or perhaps even of a gray variety, I don't mind. What matters is that for us, these more pliant ways are always more successful than the so-called standard operations. And that, more than anything, benefits our economy."

He stopped, interrupted by a stray thought. Taking out a notepad from his tight-fitting suit coat, he hurriedly jotted a few words to himself then tore out the page and stuffed it away inside an interior pocket.

"Such is the way of emerging nations," he continued. "In developed countries, the marketplaces allow little real dynamism. But in the newer places, everything is yet possible. For us, a more broadminded view of the economic framework presents a better opportunity for growth."

"Meaning that you'd rather keep all the mining illegal so you can dig yourself and control the market."

"It's our way and we've operated like this for years," he said resolutely. "Other than this past business of rooting around for gemstones, our land has remained untouched by organized commercial interests for over ninety years."

"When you say 'gray market,' I can't help but think you mean 'black market.'"

Rector Froines shrugged, not willing to quibble over such distinctions.

"In national business, a certain amount of color blindness is advantageous."

I exhaled a heavy breath. The miserable foreshadowing I'd experienced with Trevor and Stanley descended again. It was like a battering headache that returned every few hours, unwilling to release me. But with Rector Froines, there was something deeper at work. His appeal was not one that originated in public glory and ego like Trevor's, or from escapist impulses like Stanley's, but one grounded in commerce, industry, and the profit motive. As such, it radiated a kind of primal force that rendered the goals of the other men indulgent and inconsequential.

I also realized upon hearing him talk further that the implication of this had never been far away in his conversation.

"You don't want Trevor to win the election, that's why you've come," I said wearily.

Rector Froines nodded approvingly at my intuitive grasp. Whatever else the day had proved, I was becoming adept at discerning the low motives of high-minded people. His fat man's arms now were crossed determinedly in front of him, though they only made it halfway over his chest.

"Of course that's our intent, but it's more than that," he said. "It's also important that he doesn't show well, either. Really, I don't think we have to worry too much about his winning."

I failed to get this point.

"But what does it matter how many people vote for him as long as he doesn't win?"

"The better he does, the better his ideas look," said the rector. "And since he's the only one who favors ending the embargo, it would be foolish to risk that someone else won't pick up the issue to gain support. Think of it as value-added insurance. He must lose quite badly."

Rector Froines uncrossed his arms and struggled up from the soft bed, sinking backward twice before succeeding. He then drew close and laid a softball-sized hand on my shoulder. His touch was hot and damp; I felt it immediately pass through my thin cotton shirt.

"Of course, I realize this puts you in a difficult position, so naturally I'm willing to suffer some of your trouble. I'd like to triple what Trevor's paying you. In exchange, you must ensure that he performs extra poorly during this election, though that should not be difficult in itself. Of course, we'd like you to keep your job with him."

"What if I say I can't?"

"Please don't." Rector Froines's face appeared genuinely pained at my question. "This is people's livelihoods and is very serious business. There are many others who will be directly affected."

He left his hand on my shoulder a moment longer, perhaps to radiate one last quotum of malevolence, then removed it. I shivered involuntarily.

"Don't think of this as unscrupulous," he said softly. "It's merely our view of economic progress. This is how we will eventually become a First World nation. In a few generations, we shall be like you."

"Likely sooner," I said, having been defeated again.

Rector Froines brightened.

"Good. We understand one another."

I stood, automatically polite again, to show him out.

"And what am I supposed to do?" I asked.

"There's no need to worry," he said. "You'll know when the situation arises. You're American, after all."

Rector Froines went through the door, again turning sideways in order to pass. He handed me the plastic bathroom cup and paused in the hallway before leaving.

"If it makes you feel better, think of this as helping us to preserve our long-standing native traditions. Our legacies are both a record of the past and a map to the future. You can visit our agricultural basins and see for yourself their importance. If you'd like, I can arrange a tour. There have been five hundred new acres of sapodilla planted in the past six months. At night, their fragrance is quite intoxicating."

"That's all right," I said, trying to keep the shakiness out of my voice and edging the door closed on him. "I've seen your resources and I know how you feel about them. And I'm coming to understand the importance of your traditions."

XII

I WRESTLED ALL night with bad dreams. In one of them, there were far-off ringing telephones that I could not get to despite my bursting into room after empty room. In another, the image of a hideous and trussed up clown hovered and flew above me (he, too, was trying to communicate something). And in another, Sono was a yellow-jumpsuited bus driver who became increasingly angry when I could not manage the exact fare. I don't recall the ending of this figment, only my stuffing bill after bill into the bus's plastic meter box and her grimly shaking her head. Still, even in her choler I thought she looked enchanting.

I awoke tired and nerve-frayed in thrown-about sheets, thinking immediately of a well-known saying I'd come across in a detective novel (and likewise from Orozco de Basca—Declaration #17): That beyond a certain point, all dangers are equal. The distance analogy was completely apt, I thought; I felt very much trapped in a crossfire zone, vulnerable to attack no matter which way I maneuvered. And yet to stand still would be to suffer the most damage of all. I moved stiffly from the disarrayed bed and pondered my options.

After Rector Froines left, I'd spent several hours trying to invent a course of action that would somehow fulfill the demands of all those for whom I was now employed. That, of course, was sheer fantasizing brought on by my overwrought feelings of panic. But still out of nervous energy, I filled nearly three legal pads with notes and wasted an afternoon doing so.

After I finished, though, and had gloomily laid the scribble-filled ledgers next to each other on the floor, their arrangement suddenly reminded me of a swindle I had once seen on a card table in New York, one involving three coconut shells and a pistachio nut. This situation was very much like that shell game, I thought, only here it was the pea of reality that stayed in constant motion.

I then began to consider the possibility of having only one set of plans but presenting them differently so they could appeal independently to Trevor, Stanley, and the rector. This immediately felt like a more efficient, and intriguing, prospect. Instead of requiring me to create three lines of logical action, which I would then have to maintain and develop, this strategy relied on the limitless ability of people to see things as optimistically as they wished, despite circumstances. Of everything, I reflected, that was an American trait.

Emboldened, I began sketching out various ideas for a political campaign. And then it occurred to me that the best campaign might be no campaign at all. For what had hobbled Trevor in the past, I reflected, was not his style of campaign, but the fact that'd tried to wage one at all based on his ideas and proposals. Because he'd stood for something, he'd been able to be readily dismissed. Yet what if he were to have no ideas, I wondered, no beliefs beyond a simple cache of adages and slogans? What if he were to stand for absolutely nothing (beyond, of course, the standard calls to morality, civic duty, and punitive social policy), thus allowing voters to decide what they thought he stood for? It was a risky ploy—in the U. S., this sort of strategy only worked in the most important elections—but because this contest was only a few weeks off, there was a chance that it could succeed here before too many voters saw through it.

The more I considered this approach, the more its simplicity and flexibility appealed to me. Here I calculated that a campaign that deployed the most inflated and equivocal of sentiments would play to Trevor's patrician instincts of leadership, while at the same time make him a further muddle to voters already confused with choices. This Rector Froines would grasp instinctually and thus endorse; indeed, I felt confident that any strategy that relied on

Trevor's displaying a greater sense of himself in public would find immediate favor with the rector.

I then considered the different matter of Stanley and Trevor. Here I recognized that I would have to rely greatly on my persuasive ability (which by now I was quite motivated to use) to convince them of my plan's success for them. Yet here, too, I realized my way was somewhat paved, given the former's open desperation and Trevor's worsening record in public referendums. Any departure from the standard strategy had to be at least considered, and if I could point to successful American campaigns that had been run on these tactics, it was likely I could convince them of anything.

Lastly, this approach also had the very real advantage of not demanding too much of Trevor. Not only would he not be pinned down to any fixed position that he would have to acknowledge or defend, but all he needed was a half-dozen or so nonsense shibboleths that could be alliterated until they acquired some gravity of meaning. In rapid succession, I wrote down several such sayings in my notebook, inscribing them in the "FAVORITE PHRASES" folder inside my briefcase. Of them, I particularly liked, "The Voice of Reason Never Struggles to Be Heard," "Trying Times Require Trying Leaders," and "Practicing Freedom Is Everyone's Burden."

Now I dressed early and waited for Wilkie. As expected, he did not take long. Like yesterday, he arrived fifteen minutes ahead of time and spoke formally to me as we began the new day. Later on, as time passed, he would become looser in his habits but in the morning it seemed important for him to strike the appropriate tone. During the congested commute, he mentioned nothing of the day before, of Grandmama, of Stanley, or of Ponchielli. When we arrived at Trevor's house, he again hurried out of the car and pulled open the rear door so I could exit.

Trevor was sitting quietly in his strategy room when I entered. Today he was dressed more conservatively in an olive suit with a light blue shirt and a solid beige tie. Oddly, he was barefoot and his pants were rolled halfway up his legs. I understood the reason a few moments later when an elderly woman shuffled into the room carrying a large basin of foaming water and laid it on the floor in front of him. Trevor immersed his feet in the bubbling liquid and nodded his thanks to her.

"My feet are particularly susceptible to the humidity," he said after the woman left. "When I wake up in the morning, they are sometimes so swollen I cannot get out of bed."

I murmured sympathetically.

"Fortunately, Grandmama had a family recipe that cures inflammation," he went on. "My housekeeper prepares it every morning for me. It contains snakeroot, horse chestnut, and a goodly amount of coconut oil."

"Have you seen a doctor?"

"Many times. They prescribe shots that I can't abide. Grandmama's tincture is much more effective."

A sudden notion occurred to me and in my instinctual reporter's manner I tossed out a question, unconcerned over propriety.

"Your grandmother . . . is she still alive?"

"Sorry to say, she passed on years ago."

"And your parents? Do they live on the island?"

"They were missionaries," said Trevor evasively. "They died in New Guinea when I was a child. I hardly remember them. I only recall their being electrocuted in a lake during a mass baptism. They were but two of several hundred victims."

"I'm sorry."

"It's been fine," said Trevor stiffly. "I mainly feel regret for Stanley since he has the children. For them to have known their legacy would have been beneficial." He held up his dripping feet from the water as the old woman returned with a towel draped over her arm. But as she started to take away the pan, he shook his head.

"No, perhaps a little longer."

She went off with a frown and Trevor submerged his feet again.

"But this problem is not my only one," he said ruefully, changing the subject back to himself. "Lately, I have had back pains and some tremors in my wrists and chest. My physician says I'm overburdened and he's ordered me to relax my efforts. He also doesn't rule out the onset of a nerve impairment. I am well into the age when one listens extra carefully to such pronouncements."

He sighed and a portion of him seemed to give way. For the first time, I thought I glimpsed a sadness emanating from him.

"It has never been easy for me to conduct my campaigns, physically speaking," he continued. "They grow more rigorous each time, and each time I am older and less capable of meeting the demands."

He paused and looked away.

"It is for this reason that I have made a decision. I have resolved to immediately end my attempts to become president."

Later in recalling his words, what struck me most was how dumbfounded I was by them, and thus how adapted I had become to the new facts of my existence. That is, my shock over Trevor's decision truly indicated the degree to which I was ingrained in my situation. For all purposes, I was not an American tourist trapped on a meaningless tropical vacation but someone helping to direct and run a presidential campaign. This, despite my reluctance, misgivings, and despair, was now how I saw myself (and it, too, was how an increasing number of others saw me). Thus not only had I abandoned my other world but I was objecting to the imminent disappearance of this one.

"Are you sure about this?" were my first words to him.

"Absolutely. I have lain awake nearly all night. Finally I decided and it gave me peace and I fell asleep."

"Maybe you are just overtired from the campaign," I suggested.

"And if I am?" He raised his voice. "Isn't that a symptom of overall distress? Shouldn't I heed that warning for myself? I am not as young and free as you. I have to be careful with my personal resources since I have fewer of them."

I could think of nothing else to say in response and we remained silent for several moments with only the erratic groan of the air conditioner keeping us company. Now that my surprise was ebbing, a more normal sense of relief took hold of me. In terms of settling the several accounts to which I was indebted, it became clear that this was the simplest and most expedient way out. Stanley, naturally, would be agitated but my role in providing for the well-being of others now was over. The fetters were being taken off and I was becoming a free agent once more.

Lost in this happy recognition, I only gradually became aware that Trevor was speaking.

"It's not just my health," he was saying. "Perhaps it's also a realization. To be president of a nation requires much more than personal will. It's also to be singled out by destiny. I have tried twice before and I cannot see how fate would be kinder to me this time. I think there are very few among us who are ordained to rule and it is foolish to oppose those who are."

He looked steadily at me.

"I know your employment came about unusually but I hope you are not too disappointed in me. Also, I hope you understand that I cannot satisfy your retainer since my campaign has ended. However, you may keep the briefcase as a memento of my gratitude. It is quite literally all I have left to give."

Still lacking anything meaningful to say, I nodded, stood, and extended my hand. Standing up, his feet stuck in the medicine water, Trevor shook it. As he did, his left pants leg unrolled and darkened in the liquid suds.

"I understand perfectly," I said, gripping his hand firmly and shaking it in a final parting. "It's been a pleasure. I mean that truly."

XIII

WILKIE TRAILED ME out of the house and again opened the Renault's back door for me, unaware it was the last time he would have to see to my well-being. This was his final day, too, I thought, though in keeping with the caste of political campaigns, he likely would find out later. I wondered if Trevor had informed Mr. Cecilia, Mrs. Murazami, and especially Mr. Botolph of his decision, as well as anyone else he had working for him.

But I received another surprise after I settled into the backseat. Not only did Wilkie know what Trevor had said to me but he also was aware that I had not been told until just now.

"Did he give you any explanation or did he just say it's over?" he asked.

"No real reason," I said astonished and trying not to let it show.

"Me, neither. Just eyewash about his health and a lack of destiny." He looked at me in his rearview mirror. "So it's back to the hotel, then?"

I thought for a moment, reflecting on what last loose details needed to be concluded.

"Actually if you don't mind, I'd like to make one more stop."

"Of course. You want to go back to Stanley's?"

By now, I was weary of being startled by others; the constant surprises in and of themselves were becoming repetitious. I said, "Yes, please," in a neutral voice and let it go.

As I expected, Stanley was in high dudgeon when I arrived, flinging himself about his upstairs office with vehemence, opening and banging shut his windows, and throwing books and magazines whenever he happened upon them. Around me, his disturbance rained without quit for several minutes.

"I won't do it again! I won't!"

One of his smaller children appeared to deliver a message from downstairs. Stanley barked her away and slammed the door shut, triggering a fit of intense crying that he seemed not to hear. He glared at me.

"So what did he tell you? Anything?"

"The same as what he told you."

"It's not fair! He can't keep burdening me like this!"

He paused to hurl another book, a pictorial of local history, across the room. It struck a miniature family bust—of the grandmother, I think—toppling it.

"Look," I said, "even if he stayed in the race, he wouldn't have been elected. It was a long chance to begin with. Think about that part of it." I was attempting to reason with Stanley but I also was trying to cut his tirade short. Mentally, I was finished with the situation and rapidly warming to the possibilities of the rest of my vacation.

"You said yourself he was a presentable fool," I added. "And that was him at his best. How could he have won? Really, it was ridiculous."

I kept on with this kind of appeal and after a few minutes, Stanley's rants became shorter and he began to calm down. Or maybe it was that his surface anger had been spent and he now was concentrating on his deeper sentiments. Whatever it was, the room gradually quieted and he paused to rest on the couch. I noticed that for a frail man he seemed to have an ample amount of expendable energy. As for myself, however, I was feeling more and more out of place in the room. Around us, there was the violence of his discharged feelings but inside of me I was having difficulty containing my brightening emotions.

I was thus on the verge of standing up and taking my leave of Stanley and his business forever when a change came over him and he addressed me again.

"So what do you intend to do now?"

"Me? I was on vacation," I said. "I still have about a week left." I was itching to get out of the house, and perhaps inquire obliquely over Sono as well.

"You wouldn't consider staying on with me until the election?"

"Staying on?"

"There's only a short time left."

"You mean manage your campaign?"

"Not exactly. I mean just doing what you were doing."

"Doing what? Trevor's quit. He's out of the race." I was conscious of trying to keep the breezy inflection in my voice. "I believe I'm unemployed again."

"Not if you convince him back in."

"Convince him back? You mean to keep running?" His suggestion sounded both brutal and farcical and for a brief moment I could not decide which feeling to react to.

"I don't understand," I said. "He's finished with it. You talked to him yourself."

"But he only quit because he felt he had no chance. If you could get him to believe otherwise, I'm sure he would change his mind."

"I didn't get that feeling from him."

Stanley leaned forward, his eyes glinty. "If you succeed, I'll triple my retainer. And that's already double what I've already offered."

"It won't work. When someone makes a decision like that, it's not something to be taken back. It means it's over." I realized I now was struggling to keep the discussion on an unimaginable plane, even while I was annoyed at the impudence by which this proposal was being aired and the cavalier way my free time was being discussed. I defended my position by attacking his.

"How can you even pay me? Don't you already owe a lot of money?"

"Yes, and what of it?" he replied. "Public service is not that remunerative. It is inevitable that with my career and with my desires I am in arrears. But that's none of your concern. I intend to settle fully once you complete your assignment."

"But there is no assignment. He won't do it, his decision is made. It's not like he had doubts. Besides, I'm on vacation. I'm planning to see the rest of the island. I've already lost several days."

"Well, I wouldn't be so ambitious in your plans," said Stanley with an offhand grunt as he bent over and began rooting around on the floor for the nearest bottle at hand. "At least not yet."

I shivered. "What do you mean by that?"

He looked at me without expression.

"The charges against you haven't been dismissed. They're still pending. I've checked the docket."

"But Trevor said . . ."

"I'm still the vice president," Stanley interrupted harshly, "and in all matters that can concern you, I am his superior. You can be back where you were a few days ago, only with several additional counts of credit fraud and petty larceny." He smiled vaguely. "Our legal system is quite complex if it has to be."

"But this is absurd. He doesn't want to run. You can't turn that kind of thing around." I now heard outright panic in my voice.

"Certainly there's a way. The other side of pride is vulnerability. I know my brother better than anyone. He has tremendous amounts of self-worth, therefore he has to have equal volumes of the other."

"Vulnerability? He doesn't know the word."

Stanley said nothing to this, only nodded and uncapped another bottle. Watching him, it occurred to me that there are many for whom imposing their privilege is a lifelong animating force.

"It's useless," I protested, rising to my feet, "and I refuse to consider it. I'll go to the American Embassy."

"Our serious diplomatic affairs technically are still handled by France," he said. "You'll have to contact the American embassy in Paris since the office in Ryonama-Jima only handles routine concerns. The embassy is known to be efficient . . . at times."

"But you can't just lock me up. That does no one any good."

"Of course you're right."

"I'm sure the press would like this story, too. How about that for ruining his campaign? 'Candidate's Manager Jailed by Rival.'"

"Yes, they would like this news," Stanley agreed. "Over the years, they've grown accustomed to running many fantastic stories concerning my brother. Though this one probably would do more to benefit his campaign at the expense of mine."

It was impossible. I was again losing on behalf of myself. Never in my life had I made so poor a showing for my desires as in the past few days. I suddenly wondered if anything would have been different if instead of arguing I'd simply acquiesced to everything that had been put before me. Surely, at least some time would have been saved and I would be farther along in whatever string of events I'd entered into.

"But you can't reason with him," I said, grasping. "What he says or thinks, no one in their right mind understands. And I've only known him since Friday."

"Again, you raise an excellent point. You perceive things quickly and with great nuance. You'll likely do well in anticipating his needs."

"What I tell him, he doesn't respond to. I'm not even sure he likes me."

"Oh, no," said Stanley immediately. "He likes and admires you fine. He told me so himself. Who knows, there may even be a job in it for you when he wins."

"But what if I fail?"

"But you won't."

In shock, I stared around me at the torn apart room—the magazines and books on the floor, the kicked-over wastebaskets— and then at Stanley at repose on the sofa. A long minute expired. I watched its complete passing on the second hand of a crystal shelf clock that been knocked to the floor. As it wound around, it seemed to be ticking off the last of my resistance. Even the tossed-down bust of Grandmama had landed face up and seemed to be mocking me and my circumstances. I had never met such a disagreeable family, I thought. When the clock's minute hand at last circled itself, I felt drained and utterly incapable of movement.

Noting my deflation, Stanley poured out a drink and offered it to me.

"Your grandmother," I said emptily, looking at the bust and re-fusing the drink, "must have been a strong woman."

Stanley nodded.

"She was, even in death," he said thoughtfully. "You know, years ago, after Grandmama died, it was my job to dispose of her re-mains. But as I went to scatter them in the ocean, an enormous wave knocked me backwards and I ended up completely covered by her ashes. I went back into the surf but I couldn't get them off."

"What did you do?"

"I drove home and took a scalding hot shower. She was forever to rinse away."

XIV

FOR SEVERAL YEARS I have carried around a peculiar idea of happiness (peculiar in that no one I know shares it, and that when I mention my beliefs I'm usually characterized as an unhelpful depressive . . . which I'm not). At first, I assumed my ideas derived from my brief but difficult experience in marriage, but lately, I think I have always felt this way. It has just taken the aftermath of occasional hard events to develop an understanding of my feelings.

It's this: I believe that happiness exists only in the past and what serves us in the present is, at best, just distraction. Sometimes pleasant, usually not, but still, little more than contextual noise. Accompaniment we embrace as necessary for our daily routine, but all of it far short of how we envision our best days. That envisioning we reserve for our past.

This notion came to me when someone once challenged me to recall a time in my life in which I would like to have lived forever. Coming up with several possibilities was no problem. But in doing so, I realized that as I experienced these times (and in order of preference they were late college, early career, and immediate post-divorce), I was thoroughly miserable and plagued by numerous dilemmas which, I told myself, if they only would disappear, I would be happy.

Of course, no such thing happened. The problems stayed, deepened, and mostly went unresolved. A few even mutated into sources of larger unhappiness that lasted for several years. My question to my present self then became, "Why did I choose to hold these times particularly dear?" In phenomenological terms, these periods were just as harried and uneventful as the one I was living through, meaning that they were not marked by any passionate attachment to any person or thing, and nor were there any grand achievements lying in wait that could transform mine into a more exalted state (and short of inventing a badly needed vaccine or winning an Olympic medal, most of us, I think, would feel the same).

My homiletic response to this was that over time, my difficulties had bred their own appreciation. Recalling such knotty junctures in my life, I also remembered the connections that still existed with friends, the family members (and favored pets) that were still alive, and the fruitful paths of intellectual and emotional inquiry that yet lay open to me. And yes, today I would trade for all of that again in an instant . . . for the simple reason that the outcomes of all these events eventually became known to me. And given the prospect of the familiar versus that of the unknown and unexpected, I believe I will always choose that to which I am accustomed.

I know how this must sound, but my desire for the known quantity isn't what you might think. Unlike others who feel similarly about routine, I don't base my beliefs on any aversion to adventure; indeed, thanks to my itinerant economic existence, I'm quite capable of surviving in stressful situations (present one excepted, of course). Instead, my feelings result from the human hope that invariably arises with the unknown, a hope that persuades us into thinking our lives might be endowed with some measure of fulfillment—perhaps even a period or two of outright radiance—before we settle into our chosen existence.

This, of course, is a disastrous belief on many levels. In my case, for example, I can think of only one or two spectacular occasions in my forty-plus years in which my raised expectations were happily and unequivocally met. For most of us, life is generally a bout of bad sleep in which we alternately struggle to fend off the wakeful present, before sinking into a comforting communion with the remainders of the past. Indeed, I've found that to put your faith in hope is to lose your faith altogether. Even to our deathbeds, we never give up clinging to hope (Esperanza se muere ultimo/"Hope dies last"—Orozco de Basca, Declaration #8. What a terrible thought).

As I've said, mine is an odd and not altogether encouraging perspective.

However, to this I should add that even while my outlook clearly is not a useful world view since it pits one version of ourselves (the present) against another (the past) in an unforgivable equation, it still can be a reassuring way to think. For example, employing my beliefs in my current situation immediately heartened me on two levels. For one, it gave direct comfort to my spiritual state, given its iteration that since I had no expectations of being happy, unless things became unbearably bad, I probably would not become too unhappy, either. This was significant since it afforded me the guarantee of a certain degree of emotional protection.

Secondly, and in a deeper way, my thoughts also alleviated much of the feeling of circumstantial entrapment that was threatening to overtake me. Following in my customary thinking, I now could count on events following their familiar pattern of becoming more menacing than I could imagine, then receding to leave me alone and mostly unscathed, however unpleasant the actual experience proved to be. Indeed, this metaphysical schematic is one I've relied upon from adolescence to middle age—so much so, that I actually take comfort when the noisy distemper of the outside world barges into my daily existence and relieves me of the responsibility of the moment.

Of course, to most people, this sounds like classic passivity (actually, in a nutshell, it is the psychology of journalism). But that interpretation ignores the several more profound forces at work within my behavior. Rather, I prefer to think of my state not as passive, but one of active ambivalence, a condition that may have inaction as its final result but which itself is a process roiling with great emotional difficulty. For it's not from a lack of knowledge or motivation that I rely on circumstance to shape my future, it's that I suffer from too much information and thus remain searching for that last drop of data to tip the balance in favor of one action over another, a condition that I also find is becoming the *jus humanum* of our time. You might liken my state to a man busily doing nothing, only in my case even the existential pleasure of that man's absurdity is lost. And, anyway, because in the end any event can be understood in a myriad of ways, I find it all but impossible to escape the paralyzing detachment of analysis, or to keep myself from extending my ambivalence to absurd lengths.

Given this facet of my character then, did my current situation qualify as an ideal one? Well, . . . no. There were too many things wrong with it—the hard imposition of events against my will, the unpleasantness of the people involved, etc.—to allow me to be fully absorbed into it. But overall, I innately understood and appreciated its context. Perched on the rim of difficult and unasked-for circumstances, I mentally railed against their conditions while at the same time luxuriating in the release of larger self-accountability.

So where did this leave me? Unfortunately beholden once more to my original nature, I realized. Sort of happily unhappy in the manner of a tenant living in the back house on a guarded estate. The old bungalow with the erratic heat, tepid water, armies of insects, and yellowed kitchen linoleum, cracked and curling. And years from now, I will likely think of how fine the grounds actually were and how fortunate I was to be occupying them.

XV

STANLEY'S BLATHER CONCERNING his brother's psychology sounded plausible in his personally ransacked office—delivered as it was with fraternal conviction—but when I emerged in the outside world I realized that none of it would help me in persuading Trevor to alter his course. Stanley's understanding, after all, was an inbred one, and to arm myself before meeting Trevor I needed an outsider's larger perspective on the queer nature of politics here and the queerer matter of how he had managed to exist in the public consciousness (other than in a state of ridicule, that is). I suddenly recalled the name of the *Morning Gleaner* reporter and my intention to ring him up. If I did manage to convince Trevor back in the race, this would be a good time to begin an association with him; even if I failed in my mission, I could call later with the exclusive that Trevor had quit. Indeed, in spite of the harsh tone he had taken in his articles, I was glad to provide R. S. Bando with a break. Having worked and established a career in a major media market in the US, I took a superior pity on those whom I thought had been marooned on the more distant shoals of the media by bad luck, lack of ability, or their own shortness of ambition.

I asked Wilkie to stop at a newspaper box where I bought a new copy of the *Gleaner* and hunted down its address and telephone number. From a nearby phone booth, I then dialed the paper and asked for Bando. No one answered and instead I got a voicemail machine. To my surprise, it was a woman's brusque voice that told me to leave a message and the best time for her to call back. Without responding, I hung up and again called the switchboard.

"I'm trying to reach Ms. Bando. Is she in?"

I was immediately put on a very lengthy hold.

"I'm afraid she'll be back tomorrow," said the operator who I'd imagined had gone and inspected the entire newsroom and perhaps the lavatories, as well. "Do you want her message box?"

This time, I left a detailed message identifying myself and my purpose in calling, and asked that she phone me at the hotel as late as was convenient. Though I tried to sound as supplicating as possible, I also doubted that I would hear from her before the next afternoon. To a reporter, an unsolicited call is something to be put off for at least a day, or until the remindful follow-up. Some reporters are expert at never phoning back members of the public and thus manage to accomplish a great deal of work.

Returning to the car, I was uncertain how to proceed. I had hoped for some fresh information to help me plan my moves but having none threw me back on myself in an unfortunate way. I dreaded the fact that on my own I would have to convince Trevor of something firmly against his wishes, given that the act of persuading others in the service of anything but journalism has never been one of my talents. In fact, in the few times I have tried it, I've been all too amenable when people have refused what I've had to offer and more often than not, I've ended up convinced of their contrary point of view.

This lack of fervor has struck others as strange, perhaps even distasteful since it seemingly arises from a lack of resolve, yet for me it has been mostly advantageous, given that it springs from my ability to become more interested in the details of others' lives instead of the satisfying of my own desires. And perhaps it explains why so many of my news sources were so willing to talk with me and why I stayed a successful reporter for so long, at the expense, it must be said, of other callings.

Indeed, several of my colleagues, after their news careers ended, ventured into jobs in public relations and advertising. In them, they were greatly happy, working half their previous hours for a good deal more money and in the privacy of modern offices. My attempts, however, were more disastrous. Both times I tried the field, I lasted exactly three months, with my days soon deteriorating into my closing my office door, struggling haphazardly over some futile press release, then giving up and locking the door to watch the hour hand tick its way to three o'clock. At that point, I would tell my secretary that I had appointments with clients and would drive home and crawl into bed, completely worn out. From these jobs I learned the truth of the adage that it is often more exhausting to participate in the charade of work than to actually work. Invariably, too, I would wind up my long stretches of non-productivity by staring at a wallet photo of myself as a young boy and thinking that I had not been born some three decades ago to spend my days in a wood-paneled office pitching the merits of vegetable-flavored colas and Romanian automobiles to people who could care less if they heard from me or not.

Still, while the jobs lasted, I enjoyed the best pay I ever got. I missed that part.

Wilkie looked worried as I re-entered the car. It was clear that he understood something to be the matter and that whatever it was had been getting the better of me. I now recalled his rapture over the opera and was glad for the fineness of his feelings, buried under his not-so-fine exterior. I had counted him out too early as a potential helpmate and I reproached myself. His ability to know his emotions, as well as instinctively gauge the emotional gravitas of shifting conditions, was a valuable and not often found quality.

"Where to now?" he asked with concern.

"Back to Trevor's," I said reluctantly.

"Right away."

He pulled the Renault into the noisy traffic and again we were in motion, in pursuit of another heedless goal, the purpose and number of which were growing unknowable to me. As the other cars washed by us, I suddenly had the vision of myself somewhere out in the wide open, on a dirt road skimming the island littoral with the green sea on the horizon and the breezy chill of the ocean air washing over me. Perhaps at dusk in the last moments of the day's light. Back home, anyway, this was how I envisioned spending my time on this island.

I refrained from telling Wilkie this and let the notion fade as we rode along in bumpy silence. The traffic was close in, and strong tropical sunshine heated the inside of the car. Along a backed up main artery, I noticed for the first time the billboards and posters for some of the other candidates. Their ads were rabbly and cheap-looking, seemingly designed by someone who created grocery circulars. In addition, their uniform quality made it difficult to distinguish from among the candidates. This I would have to change when it came to Trevor, I thought.

When we got to the house, Wilkie turned to face me.

"If you don't mind, I'll wait outside," he said. "I might say something that wouldn't be right. I was getting paid extra for driving and I was counting on it. At least he could have warned me."

I nodded.

"I may be a while."

"Then I'll park over there." He indicated a squat frame house on which hung a tattered sign that advertised cigarettes, beer, packaged foods, and tickets for that day's national lottery, the prize for which was roughly 170 US dollars.

I left him in the running car and went up to knock at Trevor's. After several moments, a frail figure appeared behind the screen door. Gradually, I recognized the old woman who had fetched the water for Trevor's feet.

"Did you leave something?" she asked in an unfriendly manner.

"I've come to see Mr. MacGower."

"He's resting. He asked me not to wake him." Through the darkened shade, I saw her body go rigid with opposition.

"But it's urgent and I need to speak with him immediately. If you don't wake him, he's liable to become very upset." I added, "I wouldn't have come otherwise."

She stared at me a long moment and then, muttering, lifted open the latch on the screen and went off. I entered into the same dense gloom as that morning, this time blinded further by the sudden scattering of dust motes that flew off the dirty mesh. From a back room, I heard a rumbling and scraping movement, and then a sharp, raised voice. Then Trevor appeared, his bulk garbed ludicrously in a powder blue caftan that fell to his ankles and hung off his flabby man's shoulders and breasts.

His look was one of dark suspicion.

"I was resting," he said crossly. "I'd just settled in."

"I'm sorry but I need to speak with you. Can we go to your office?"

I was aware that my forward demeanor took him by surprise. However, it must have made an impression for wordlessly he turned and began angrily leading the way to his musty room, the ridiculous robe billowing behind like a child's parachute. As I followed, I stepped carefully around the house's many fragile furnishings and the thin, slippery throw rugs that threatened to upend me in the dim hallways. Back inside his office, I saw that it had been left as earlier, with the used glasses on the table and the plastic tub of balm still on the floor. The snakeroot or horse chestnut had rotted in the water and filled the air with a rank scent.

Trevor settled himself quickly in a chair and without waiting for me to do likewise, began speaking.

"All right, what is it that you have to say?" His manner tried to remain stormy but I could tell that he was curious as well over my intentions. This was an aspect of my character he had not foreseen.

"I've come to change your mind," I said evenly. "I think you should reconsider your decision and stay in the race."

He snorted.

"How forceful of you to come and put it like that. I thought I made myself clear this morning."

"Yes, but I didn't have a chance to respond. If I can, I think you're throwing away an extraordinary advantage."

"How so?" Comfortable now and wide awake, he became humorously interested and even receptive to my appeal, given that I now was playing to his larger sense of himself.

"Just this. After we spoke, I went to the library and looked at the newspaper coverage of your other campaigns. Really, it wasn't your fault you didn't succeed in them. I simply think that you weren't properly understood in either one."

Years as a reporter had taught me a valuable trait: how to speak effortlessly on my feet without worrying where the next turn of phrase might come from or lead to (any self-consciousness, in fact, would rupture the trance line of communication). Instead, all this kind of spontaneous articulating required was the ability to fully grasp the situation in front of you, while at the same time to use the feelings and words of people against themselves. Now I relied on this state of free associating to argue my case with enthusiasm and alertness, only making sure to drive home one underlying point: that Trevor's defeats were in no way connected to his beliefs or political thinking.

"Yes, I have considered that as well," said Trevor, the barest edge of conviction entering his voice. "That feeling in itself is what has enabled me to run again and again. But I have no evidence the people now are more willing to modify their views of me."

"If I can be blunt," I said, "it's not up to them to correct their misimpressions. In this you have failed, too. People need a certain amount of guidance so that they might see your purpose for them. Otherwise, they remain confused."

My answer again surprised him but only for the moment.

"And how would you guide them?" he snapped. "And mind you, I'm only listening. For the first time in two months, I have enjoyed a midday sleep and the pain in my feet is subsiding."

His glare was returning.

"Let me tell you about journalists and how they are taught to function," I began. "Though they may not acknowledge it, most of them learn to imagine the world in very simple terms. If they don't, there's no room for them in the profession. Take any story—say a gang shooting, a reunion of old lovers, or one about struggling immigrants. In the professional reporter's hands, they become tragedy, fate, and hope, respectively. Simple emotions, judgments, and moralities. To write up events in the basest of terms is what makes for a successful journalist. Complications anger editors. They'd rather not know about them first of all, and after awhile, they forget they exist."

"Yes," said Trevor vaguely. "The press can be a problem." He was not at all aware as to where I was leading him, but rather following like a large animal trundling after an encouraging scent.

"Your problem is that you've become overly involved," I went on. "But the press wants less, not more, explanation. The media actually are in a revolt against knowledge. They only pretend to embrace it. They really want nothing more than the comfort of their own views and to be left alone to put out the story. They have dozens of others to get to, why should they invest too much time into yours? To believe otherwise is foolish."

I stopped and looked directly at Trevor and in the contours of his overdeveloped features, I began to witness something I had not seen before. As I watched, his inner frailties seemed to slowly materialize and declare themselves on his face (and I read them to be a haunting lack of self-esteem, as well as an inability to correctly process the meanings of human interaction). But in a clarifying instant, I also saw this pose would be powerfully effective. Because of it, people would trust him since they could not foresee any other hidden defects of his behavior.

"So what is your point?" he asked impatiently. "How should I behave?"

"Forget your proposals for change and your solutions to problems," I said. "Rely instead on the force of your personality. That's what people really want to know about. Once you've convinced them of yourself, everything else will be free for you to decide. You'll have the upper hand."

"Surely it can't be as simple as that?" he exclaimed. "Has it been that the voters just haven't known me?"

In his voice, wonderment had caught up to and now was overtaking his doubt.

"Speak straightly to them," I instructed. "People have to be directed into their beliefs. What occupies you is what will capture them. Capitalize on your established position. Speak of your roots, your tradition and history here. How many others are there like you? There is only Stanley and once people have deduced that, then it's between the two of you."

"He is a much better politician," Trevor said for protest's sake. "Better at negotiating skillful advantages."

"And let the people see that," I answered, "and then let them see how you are. Your personality will be the difference. To entertain the public in the service of improving it is no disgrace."

He was silent for a long time. When he spoke again, his words came low and rapid, as if he could not trust his emotions in the higher registers of expression.

"What will I have to do?" he asked. "What do you propose?"

"First a big staging."

I stumbled and halted abruptly. Truly, I had no idea as to where I was headed with this part and the sudden request for a specific course of action brought me up short. All I had meant to do was allude to a campaign that could encompass Trevor's incoherencies and aberrations and make it seem as if they had some kind of overall purpose. But then, like sitting behind the wheel of a powerful automobile, I mentally let go the clutch and went barreling forth again.

"You must first imprint your image into the minds of the people," I said firmly. "The rest of the candidates are a pack. You must break free of their dismal causes and rants."

I saw this pleased him so I went on.

"Conceive of yourself not as a leader but as a force. Let the others stand for policy and analysis. Let them compare poorly by their own dreadful discussions."

"Yes, yes," he concurred.

"Let your expression form your beliefs. Be willing to have no purpose, no plans, no ideas. Nothing whatsoever. The key to success is to not entertain its possibility."

"Then what should I speak about?"

"Show the people your unshakable faith in them and in their inherent strength and dignity. It's time for bold leadership to unite the country. I would think that someone from your tradition would have no trouble defending this ideal."

"Of course that's what I stand for," he said strongly. "It is part of my heritage."

"Throw off all campaign trappings and hold no press confer-. ences and prepare no speeches. Simply talk at the moment, of the moment. And hold nothing back when you do."

"Yes, yes. That is perhaps my finest talent."

"Go about each event as if the election were just a few minutes away. Plunge forward into the hearts of the people. Let them embrace you."

"If it's what they want, I've no choice."

"Resist the cheap debate and the arguments of the others. Remain fast to your visions. Refuse to be dragged downward with your opponents."

"It will be a relief. I've never liked the political discourse and then the endless campaigning over ideas. Despicable and wearisome."

"Be yourself. Above all, display your character. Let the others and their concerns be judged against you and yours."

"There's nothing they can score me with."

"It's not an election, it's an attempt to change the nation. You can't lose for yourself, you can only succeed for others."

"The moment is here. I shall do whatever it takes."

"I can't tell you how that makes me feel," I said.

XVI

I RETURNED TO my hotel room early that evening. After leaving Trevor's, I rode around the island in search of relief, looking for a place that would match the bucolic, windswept scene that I had imagined back home in my city apartment. But after nearly two hours toiling along one-lane roads that kept a long distance from any coastal stretches, I told Wilkie to turn around and we started back.

Along the way, I began to confide to him some of what had transpired between Trevor and me. As he was about to be employed again at extra pay, he was heartened by the developments and in my role in fostering them. I could tell in his easy yet wary manner that he felt the good judgment he had invested in me somehow had paid off. And though I didn't inform him about the bottom-line nature of my intentions, I also felt Wilkie now knew enough to qualify as a partial confederate in my planning.

In my room, I then phoned Rector Froines and Stanley. To the former, I related my conversation with Trevor and the absurd manner I'd outlined for his undoing. To Stanley, I related the same exchange and the plan I'd conceived for Trevor's change of heart and his eventual triumph. Given that people usually are more willing to put their belief in the frankly unbelievable, and that many areas of life are not governed by plausibility but by whether something is implausible enough to be true (there is religion, after all), Stanley proved easier to assure than Rector Froines, though the minister, too, eventually became convinced of my plan's potential.

There also was a message from Ms. Bando. I ordered an exorbitant room service steak and a pot of coffee and called her back.

"You're the man Trevor hired," she said immediately. "Is it true he's quitting?"

"Absolutely not. We're full-steam ahead and looking forward to the campaign."

"What about the latest polls? What does he intend to do about those?"

"In fact, I've just come from a strategy session where we've devised a new platform to stir every voter in Momo-Jima. No one will be unmoved. If you'd like, I can give you the preview."

"Better hurry with it, there's not much time left."

Her voice was snappish but had an agreeing lilt to it. I realized I now was talking to the journalist that I had been so often in my life, and that I was defiantly on the other side. It triggered a queasy feeling.

"Shall we meet?" I asked. "I know you'll find our latest direction exciting. I can send a car, if you'd like."

"That may be hard. I've got four other candidates to corral and an election overview to manage. I'm all alone on this since the intern was quarantined for monkeypox."

"But just briefly then. I'm giving it to you first. Ten minutes Thursday for coffee?"

"Ten minutes won't do me any good to get to know you, and if you've really got something for me, ten minutes won't be enough."

But she paused and I heard her turning some quick pages.

"Well Thursday's no good. It's National Public Works Day. All the roads will be closed." I heard more hasty rustling.

"What about tomorrow? Say eleven at your hotel. There's a small restaurant there, I think."

"The restaurant at eleven is fine."

"I can't stay long, I promise you. Unless you've got something truly worthy."

"If it's truly worthy, as it is, you won't mind," I responded quickly. "And if it's not, then it's only ten minutes."

"I suppose. How will I know you?"

"There won't be many people there. But I'll be carrying a leather briefcase. A new one."

"I'll wear yellow," she said decisively. "And sunglasses, as well. We'll see each other."

"Good. Looking forward to it."

"Me too," she said. Then, with a hint of mischievousness, she added, "You did see our editorial yesterday? 'How the Dumber Brother Should Be Smothered'?"

Though I knew she meant it as a shot to test my character (or to show hers as a journalist), her remark still bothered me, though not on the level she intended. Instead, I didn't care for the juvenile sound of the headline, nor for her quick, size-it-up reporter's way of saying it.

"I must have missed it," I said stiffly.

"No one reads anymore," she said with discernible resignation toward the vast uninterested public, which in her mind now included me. "I'll bring a copy and maybe you can give me a quote in response. Maybe that will make for a story." She then said good-bye and hung up.

———

The next morning, I went early to the restaurant to pick out a comfortable and strategic table. One that would not have the sun beaming in my face as I spoke and one large enough to let me display the campaign materials I wanted her to see. Also, despite that it was only a business meeting, I felt compelled by the cardinal rule never to keep a woman waiting, especially at a restaurant.

But as soon as I entered the empty dining area, I saw that she already had commanded the advantage and was seated in a shady window booth with a notebook and several newspapers spread out in front of her. As I approached, she removed her sunglasses.

"What are you doing here?" I asked incredulously.

"My breakfast appointment was cancelled so I came early to eat," said Sono Bando. "I was starving."

"Never mind that. You're R. S. Bando? You didn't mention it on the phone."

"I thought you knew who you were talking to," she said lightly. "You're the campaign manager, right?"

"You didn't say anything at Stanley's. And I'm not the manager."

She shrugged.

"What was I supposed to say besides 'hello'? You don't go around spilling yourself to people you've just met."

"No, but isn't this a breach of interest? You're related to Stanley. How can you write about him?"

"I'm related to Nao, not him," she said archly. "She's my half-sister. Besides, I can't stand Stanley so if they're looking for a critical stance on him, they've got one from me."

I was flummoxed. Of the many improbabilities I had walked through in the last several days, this was the utmost of my surprises. Yet at the same time, I was aware of the small shaft of pleasure that was wending its way through me. I recalled that she had been in my dreams and once people are in your dreams, you never regard them the same. I considered this, and the dream, for a moment, then came back to attention when I realized she had been talking.

"It really is a small island," she was saying. "Everyone who runs things knows one another, or they should. I was a reporter before Stanley married Nao so why should I have to quit?"

"Surely it must get in the way at times. And don't people object?"

"I'm very careful when it comes to politics. And besides, this sort of problem only comes around every three years. In between, it's crime and weather stories."

"I see."

Sono noticed my lack of a meaningful answer.

"Would you rather not meet if it makes you uncomfortable?" she asked. "There're four other candidates and all of them probably deserve the coverage more than Trevor."

"No, of course not," I said, changing my manner. "I'm just surprised, that's all. What would you like to know?"

"You asked me here."

"Oh, right."

I opened my briefcase and began fumbling inside. As I did, I suddenly decided not to take out the detailed itinerary I'd lined up for Trevor (and which I was going to let Sono peruse off the record), nor any of the comparison points I'd made between him and the other candidates. Instead, all I removed was a single piece of paper upon which were written the new precepts on which Trevor's campaign would now be based. Though they consisted only of a few paragraphs—emphasizing the concepts of "destiny," "nation-building," and "moral duty"—it was an extremely difficult piece of writing; I had stayed up past midnight getting the wording exactly right.

"That's a very nice attache," she said.

"Yes, he gave it to me when I joined up."

"Trevor's like that. He starts off big so people are made to feel grateful but then he refuses to give them any money or recognition. Stingy is what he really is. He recruited you in jail, didn't he?"

"Yes," I said, irritated at her impertinence. Is this what journalists were really like?

"Well, then you're probably better than the other advisors he's had. There was one who was insane, certifiably so. He broke down in the middle of a campaign and got packed off to a clinic in Jakarta. Then there was the Harvard man who came down on vacation and got swept into it like you. He was the most inept of them all. He wasn't very smart but he was tall and for awhile that fooled everyone. Strange, isn't that, that good universities have the luxury of graduating dunderheads? Especially if they're above average height."

I had no response to this and simply gave her a tight smile (or grimace). Not only was it discomfiting to be in the company of a working reporter, but it also was unnerving being with such a chatty one who so easily ran down my own conversation.

I handed her the sheet of paper. "Here is our new campaign strategy," I said. "We're keeping it simple and focusing on these messages. We want to avoid the sorts of arguments that could tie up voters' minds."

She took the paper and I watched her read. Suddenly she burst out laughing.

"Why, you've decided to run him as an outright buffoon," she laughed. "Oh, that's lovely."

I started to object but her straightforward and spontaneous laughter defeated me. And after a few awkward moments, I made a gesture of surrender with my palms and acquiesced. And then the feeling of pleasure that I was carrying over her grew stronger. Like Wilkie, she had partly joined my ranks of conspirators, a secret society whose numbers I realized with welcome surprise, were growing.

"Well, is it any less likely he'll get elected this way?" I asked.

"No, not at all," she said, still laughing. "In fact, I think he's got a decent chance now. More so than he's enjoyed in the past. Stanley will be pleased, at any rate. This really is a precious document."

I suddenly grew worried.

"You're not going to write it like that, are you?"

"Of course not," she said sharply, as if correcting a child. "This is still the news media. We can't get away with that sort of truth-telling. Besides, now there's a chance that Trevor could get some actual support and that would make things more interesting. You were quite clever to come up with this sort of angle."

I beamed inwardly at her words, feeling as incandescent as one does when receiving unrestrained praise from an attractive woman. Emboldened, I took the sheet back from her fingers and looked at her directly.

"You don't think people will catch on to this?"

"Some might but they won't believe it. Everyone's much too used to Trevor's acting the fool. Nothing rational has come out of his mouth, ever. They almost expect this sort of thing from him, even without him saying it."

"But how will that make him successful?"

"Well, it stands to make him more distinct, won't it? The rest of the candidates are the same—a dull, depressing bunch. They couldn't manage the entrance to a men's room. When Stanley's won, it's been by default."

"What about you? Don't you have any preferences?"

"Absolutely none," she said. "I'm concerned only for Nao. She's unhappy that Stanley's unhappy. So in that sense, I suppose I hope your scheme does strike gold. It would solve their problems."

She fell quiet, still laughing a bit, reflecting perhaps on the odd arrangements that events often have to take in order to bring happiness to people. And in an unrelated way, I found myself thinking the same kinds of thoughts. I folded the paper into my pocket and caught her eye.

"One more thing," I said. "With the new focus in our campaign, I'll need to keep you apprised of our developments. Maybe quite often with the sort of last-minute rush we're putting on."

Sono allowed herself a half-smile.

"Oh, I expected that," she said tartly, gathering up her newspapers as the waitress came with her order. "But you've got my number now and you know where to reach me. All I ask is that you call me first."

Part Two

XVII

A WEEK WENT by. I was now working hard and anticipating the onset of imminent exhaustion. Nightly, I returned to my hotel around one or two a.m., winded after a hard day of intricate scheming and public orchestrations but oddly, also brimming and rampant with ideas for the next. One morning a radio speech with paid boosters and canned effects, the next day a parade of supermarket and rest home appearances, then returning press calls that evening and dreaming up slogans for billboards and banners . . . it was a temporary madness state I'd entered into. I felt a sort of bottomless electricity powering my thinking and I refused to budget my attention to anything not related to the hectic dispensation of duties and events. I now traveled with a cellular phone and pager, ate irregularly and badly, and kept two full sets of clothes in the car, for it also grew unbearably hot during this time. I also filled a half dozen reporter's notebooks with my notes and impressions, as well as a multiplying list of names of those who promised help and money, as well as their schedules and phone numbers and a running total of how much we'd gotten from them and how much had been pledged all together (when I truly throw myself into something, even unwanted assignments, I submerge completely. Later, in recalling my fervor, I frighten myself).

What kept me in such a state? Well, for one, I was being badly ground up in the machinery of proliferating details. In all the elections that I'd been privy to, there were usually many people attending to the sort of minutiae that now filled my time. Here, however, the scheduling of appearances, as well as the bus rental the next afternoon, the refrigerating of drinks and sandwiches, the arranging for the hundreds of folding chairs, etc. were solely my concerns. Tending to the growing press inquiries and making copies of speeches, brochures, and fliers also took hours each day. And since I was the one who'd convinced Trevor back into the race, it fell to me alone to take on these jobs, his small retinue of supporters having fallen away with his original decision. In retrospect, I'm afraid, I drove poor Wilkie particularly hard during this time, though he was never less than well-humored and helpful, even in the midst of onerous errands, hours of traffic, and days that began at six a.m.

I also kept in touch with Sono, though not as frequently as I'd envisioned. She was greatly occupied with the other candidates, as well as with the occasional assignments that broke through the continuous wall of political coverage, and had little time for anything but brief communiques. I did sense, however, that her thoughts had shifted favorably in my direction; that is, since my immediate job of making Trevor president also fell within her wishes, whenever I did call, she seemed glad to hear from me. It was at the hard end of another day, in fact, when I phoned her office to leave a message and she unexpectedly answered, that I suggested we meet for coffee.

"It's too late for coffee," she said, her keyboard audible in the background as we spoke. "How about drinks?" Without waiting for my reply, she named a place and told me to wait for her.

Twenty minutes later, we were seated in a dark booth at the Dunbar-dori Airport lounge, a spot where she thought we would be left alone from those who might see us and interrupt us either with work or their company. She ordered a rum and diet cola and began smoking from a pack of ultra-light mentholated cigarettes.

"It's going well for you, isn't it?" she asked. "They say you're getting actual turnouts these days."

In the bar's dim light, I could see her automatically taking out her notebook and pen.

"Better and better. Maybe you should see for yourself."

She shook her head.

"Can't. Trevor still doesn't have a chance. It's Stanley and Van Gland they want, at least until the numbers change."

"When does your next poll come out?"

"Day after tomorrow, along with analysis."

"You may be surprised."

"It'd be nice to think so." She mashed out a cigarette and began another. "But if you've got something worthwhile, maybe I can ask for a few hours on it."

I responded at once, having finalized most of the next day's schedule on the drive over.

"Tomorrow he's at the fish market in the morning," I began, "a rubber glove factory in the afternoon, and then having lunch with a French Empire Patriots group in Konoki. I don't know what we've got yet for the evening. But the fish market should be good color. Seven a.m. at the port landing."

"Don't drag me out of bed for that. Please."

"How about sending a photographer in the morning and then covering the lunch? It's at the Millipedist's Club."

"I'll ask but I don't think they'll go for it. Other than for nov-elty's sake, Trevor doesn't register with the editors. They've been through this before."

"They're missing a story. He got an ovation today at the correc-tional facility. Everyone stood for over a minute."

"Who scheduled him there?" She blew a cloud of smoke in dis-belief. "Prisoners don't vote. And it's not like they could walk out."

"His idea. He's not campaigning, remember? He's only speaking the truths that others dare not mention."

"Sorry. Was this the 'Standing Up for Your Right to be Momo-Jiman' talk or the new one on 'Freedom of Destiny'?"

"The latter."

"Odd place to be talking about or freedom or destiny, don't you think? So maybe there was a story."

She finished the rest of her drink, ground out her cigarette, and lit another. She smoked seemingly compulsively, though only puff-ing halfway through a cigarette before striking up the next. This contradictory habit, too, made her appealing.

"All right," she said after thinking a moment. "I can try to get a piece in. Moatley is fading and Bergeron's wife is threatening to divorce him unless he quits so you won't see him after next week. It's really Stanley versus Van Gland and in a two-man race a little comic relief can't hurt."

I let her remark pass. Instead, I finished my beer and took one of her cigarettes.

"We're buying TV spots, did I tell you? Trevor now feels that television is his most natural medium. He now wants someone filming him all the time."

"No." She was surprised. "Where did you get the money?"

"Well, from Stanley, among others. They start airing Wednesday and run until election day. Ten a day on all three channels."

"What do they look like?"

"Mainly stills with narration. We recorded two this morning. Wilkie, the man who drives me around, did the speaking. He's got quite a voice, a real *basso profundo*. Like the voice of the inner earth."

She murmured admiringly.

"That's a step forward. But if I were really interested in pursuing it, I'd ask who the 'among others' are."

"You may have to become interested. If anything should happen to Van Gland, like a blown comment or an ex-girlfriend (or boyfriend), then it's Stanley's race to lose. And don't think he wouldn't try."

"I hadn't thought of it like that," she admitted. "But then I'm not conditioned to be optimistic about these things."

The waitress came and we ordered more drinks. Sono paid with bills from her purse—the reporter's prerogative—and looked at me pensively.

"You're not at all worn down by this, are you? You sound pretty lively, even with all your hours. Sleep deprivation actually seems to agree with you."

"Actually, I'm exhausted but I'm feeling fine," I answered truthfully. "I seem to have lots of energy even though I'm not sure where it all comes from."

The strength in my voice surprised me. I recognized that in her absent-minded but reflexive probing, Sono had sprung in me an undetected well of emotion. I went on.

"It is strange. Sometimes I feel like I've been bounced from the real world and gotten plugged into something that's made me forget all about who I am. I really haven't thought about anything in my normal life for days. And for it to happen here, an island on the edge of nowhere, drifting from sunset to sunset . . . Once in a while, I try to let it all sink in, but it hasn't."

Immediately, I could see from Sono's face that I might have gone too far since my words could also be implied as commenting upon her presence here as well. Nevertheless, what I'd said was true and would continue to be true as long as the island stayed above sea level. The world is extraordinarily full of aimless realms that have dropped their tethers to it and this was just one of them.

And to imagine that many people spend their lives dreaming of retiring to such places is also extraordinary.

"Lucky for you that you got us during an election," Sono said coolly. "Otherwise you'd just be watching us gather seaweed or pile sandcastles. We're not always this entertaining."

I reddened slightly. I'd forgotten that journalists can never be neutral, as they pretend to be; it is only another of the many self-imposed fallacies they need to do their kind of work. Of everyone I'd known, reporters tended to be the most privately partisan of people, probably because of the tyranny of objectivity that always oversaw their official dealings.

"I didn't mean it like that," I said hastily. "It's just that I didn't expect to become so involved in things in a place like this. I came here to get away from everything like that."

"We're not a joke, you know," Sono said irritably. "Just because our life here doesn't match what you're used to doesn't mean we're disposable."

"No one said you're disposable." I felt a resentment rise in my voice. "But some of the customs here are a little unusual. What about this whole election? I've never heard of anything so convoluted. Surely you must see that."

"I suppose, from your viewpoint. But are we any odder than where you're from? Every time I read about your country, I hear about all the strange people you put in office with all their strange ideologies and I think where following them has gotten you." Sono finished her drink as the waitress came back and distributed the fresh round.

"Really, what makes us any worse?" she continued. "I have no illusions about this island but I've spent a few years abroad, too. What they cook up in those places sent me screaming back here. Imagine, walls to separate people from murdering each other or blowing up countries to save them. At least our indulgences are harmless. We're not rounding up people or torturing innocents."

"But that's impossible here. What would you fight over? Who would you round up? It seems ridiculous even to imagine." Caught up in the moment, I temporarily forgot my own state.

"It's not that we can't be horrible, too," she answered. "It's just that in the bigger places, you need bigger mechanisms to get things done. But once you've set them up, they can't help but produce the wrong results. Look at how wars get started. They all come out of big, rational systems set up by terribly rational people to prevent them from ever happening. And still they don't stop, and even worse, when they do, everyone just goes along as if they've got no choice. That's your sane view of things."

"But there's plenty of brutality in smaller countries, too," I said. "Usually more so, given that no one's really looking or cares."

Sono sighed. Her cigarette had exhausted itself in the ashtray. Again she had burned more than she smoked.

"You're still more of a journalist than you'd like to think," she said. "You'd rather sum up than try to understand. This is a complicated world run by crazy, ill-minded people. I just want to find the least complicated spot I can and see things from there. Is that such a bad thing?"

"No, but how much can you see here? Don't you miss the bigger view?"

Sono looked at me with a sense of pity, one eyebrow arched above the other like a wave poised to crash.

"Bigger view of what? Of unhappiness and misery? I'm lucky to have the choice so I prefer to focus on things that are less awful, thank you. It's only the most innocent mind that chooses to orbit around the worst that life offers. Spare me that indulgence. Besides, I like the familiarity I have here. I don't have to explain myself every time I go out in the world, nor have the world explain itself to me. What's so wrong about trying to live your life to scale? What about your life? Are you always that happy living in a big city? And tell the truth."

"No, I'm not always happy," I said, "but living in a city isn't about always being happy. Living in a city is about what might be available to you. It's about possibility, even if it usually doesn't work out."

"And you're used to that possibility not working out?" she asked. "You can live with your disappointments?"

"Generally, I ignore them."

"And that works for you?"

"Yes, but—"

"But what?"

"But there's a catch. The less aware you become of your discontent, the less aware you become of your desires. Until finally you're so successful that you've forgotten what it was that you wanted. But what you want also constitutes who you are. So in the end, you can kind of disappear if you're not careful."

"You strike me as being too scrupulous to let that happen."

"And there's the other thing," I went on. "If you've forgotten what it is you're supposed to remember about yourself, how do know who you once were? Maybe an occasional glimpse or a thought of 'I used to enjoy that' or 'I used to be like that.' But at the time you recall it, the memory seems so foreign it might as well belong to another person. Then sometimes . . ."

"I'm sorry, the advantage to this existence is . . . what?" interrupted Sono. "It seems like such an absurd condition to defend. Are you being at all serious? I've never ever considered my life on these terms and hope I never have to. Is this what city life is like for you?"

I waited a moment before answering, studying Sono's face in the dim light. And as I did, it occurred to me how easy, and pleasurable, it would be to overcome my objections and simply agree with her. Not because of what she was arguing but for the feeling of it. Love, I suddenly recalled, is creating complete agreement (Orozco de Basca—Declaration #20).

"All right, maybe I was trying to be serious, if not honest," I said, relenting. "Maybe I should expand my boundaries of appreciation. It could be I am overlooking some significant things here."

"Well, thank you, and I'm flattered to hear it. Next you're going to compare me favorably to a brisk walk by the ocean or the pleasures of a cut field of grass. I could be at home now, you know. I don't exactly have the luxury of much sleep these days."

Now it was the strength in her voice that surprised me.

"Are you telling me this is more than just professional?" I asked.

"You know perfectly well what I'm telling you."

"I didn't realize we were being so friendly."

"I can't figure out what you realize and what you don't."

"I'm only trying to say what I feel."

"Now you are beginning to annoy me," she said and lit another cigarette.

XVIII

My meetings with Trevor, on the other hand, were not so re-warding. Having seen a greater reaction to his new public identity, he soon became convinced of his own politic value and thus wished to engage me more and more in weighty analyses of matters that were utterly foreign to him: international monetary relief, ethnic terrorism, the problems of state religions, et al. It was odd—the more freely he associated while speaking in public, the more nar-rowly he tried to attack particular issues in private. Though I man-aged to limit these new sorts of diatribes to no more than thirty or forty minutes (usually by harkening back to the campaign's foun-dational themes and his role in orchestrating them), they were still torturous to endure and made my immediate chores harder. Never was his position over me exposed more cruelly than by his ability to hold me against my will in these discussions.

"Perhaps that's what makes us either conservatives or liberals," he said one morning a few days after my meeting with Sono. He held up a magazine.

"Here's someone who writes that conservatives lack remorse be-cause they believe that some people have an innate and permanent privilege, no matter how unearned. I agree with that assessment but I've also observed that liberals desire the reverse. They often wish to absorb an undue dread in order to justify their comfort. So against both of these fallacies, I propose an alternative: the utter and complete freedom from the burden of ever having to earn anything. It is the evolution of a new social contract."

Given that this line of discourse was more interesting than most of his thoughts (and also that I was not opposed to this way of thinking, and told him so), for once I was reluctant to break him off. However, I also wanted to turn his attention to a television debate I'd tentatively scheduled with his rival Bergeron. I felt the exchange would do much to bolster Trevor's standing while at the same time dethrone his opponent's waning legitimacy.

But when I brought it up, he was dismissive.

"Oh that. Cancel it. I'm better off resting and saving myself for the weekend," he said. "I'm doing too well now to be concerned with the likes of him."

Though abrupt, Trevor's response was accurate. For he was do-ing well now, much better than anyone could have foreseen even a few short days before. The *Gleaner's* poll had since come out and placed him third among the candidates, trailing Stanley and Van Gland by only a dozen percentage points. It was a finding that shocked all the campaigns, as well as the dwindling members of the public who still cared about the election (voter turnout was be-ing pegged at about fifteen percent, and even that was an optimistic presumption). Moreover, though he still was lagging significantly, at least it could now be said that Trevor was within far-sighted striking distance of the frontrunners and at that, he was elated.

How this sudden upward movement occurred was remarkable and yet predictable. Simply, it followed the course of most modern cultural phenomena. That is, it was a meaningless event that filled a waiting public vacuum and by dint of mass attention acquired signif-icance, then urgency. It went according to the laws of the present-day consumptive media and it was fortunate for Trevor that my back-ground was in this and that I could take advantage of the mecha-nism's unfailing ability to embody nothing yet signify everything.

For example, early on, given the meager numbers of probable voters and the potential of the election to turn on the support of a committed few, one strategy that immediately suggested itself to me was to isolate Trevor in himself. Meaning that, as a candidate,

Trevor (under my direction) began appearing completely indifferent to the courting of any mass favor or attention, while at the same time offering no overtures or meaningful answers to voters or reporters. Standing alone as a matter of choice, not circumstance, which is how it usually had been. Trevor quickly grasped the ease of this technique and took it to heart so strongly during interviews and rallies that his disregard for others bordered on rudeness, so intent was he on acting out in the spirit of the moment.

Initially, this stance gave the campaign a boost since it served to separate Trevor from the other candidates, even if only from the standpoint of novelty. However, Trevor's continued refusal to engage in any sort of electoral dialogue, coupled with the abstruse pronouncements that he put forth as his "platform," piqued a genuine public interest and his isolationist pose soon gave way to an absolutionist one. Almost overnight, the perception became that Trevor was addressing areas of vital concern in a new and fundamental way, not just speaking in unraveling bouts of absurdity. Indeed, given that he appeared to controvert all that was sensible in politics and public behavior, everywhere he went more and more people came to see him, first from a casual, almost freakish interest, then impelled by their sense of him as a late-breaking and significant phenomenon.

Thus in the manner of a week to a week and a half, the notion of Trevor's candidacy evolved into a legitimate event, something that people now attended to, discussed, and felt they needed to partake in. For having committed itself, the public then clamored for its counter-right to share in and shape the moment (and fortunately for us, I thought, the election would be over soon enough so that people would not have a chance to tire of him). Unsolicited boosters and small but turbulent crowds increasingly greeted Trevor's appearances, and I became even more hard-pressed to keep up with the growing maze of logistical details and conflicting demands of campaign minutiae (here, Mr. Cecilia, Mrs. Murazami, and Mr. Botolph returned to the fold and gave me needed help). I also began to spend more and more time managing the press coverage that had materialized in the wake of the *Gleaner's* poll. Daily, I shunted

Trevor in front of reporters for whom he was invariably prickly and impatient, berating them long after they shut their notebooks and clicked off their recorders. This, however, only further heightened their appraisal of him as a meaningful development, which in turn prompted more coverage.

Still, though, I could not feel wholly free in enjoying the crescendoing travesties I was orchestrating. To wit: Trevor's dramatic gains now greatly worried Rector Froines. He made the point several times to me by telephone and once he sent his assistant, Mr. Brunt, a tall Chinese man with high marcelled hair, to a rally as a visible and implacable reminder of my duty to his side of things. But though I did my best to calm the rector, Trevor's rapidly improving situation was rendering all my efforts futile and I found myself having to invent new and increasingly bizarre excuses for his success. Indeed, the only thing that saved me for awhile was when I reiterated to the rector the essential fatuousness of Trevor's campaign, the intent of which he completely understood and agreed with. But that Trevor was winning support infuriated him and eventually Rector Froines changed his approach with me, too.

One morning, his car—an old-style, wood-paneled station wagon—appeared outside a diner where Trevor was holding court with a group of other lesser-known religious leaders. Mr. Brunt came inside and on seeing him, I excused myself from the stenchy restaurant and went out to talk with the rector.

"It's no good," he said gravely as we sat in the back seat of the station wagon. "You'll have to convince him to quit. There's no other way. I'm losing sleep and my wife says I get up five or six times a night blaspheming. I can't have it."

That Rector Froines was married surprised me more at the moment than his new orders to me. He shifted his great bulk and the car moved with it.

"But he can't possibly win," I protested. "He's doing better but still not enough to beat Stanley or even Van Gland. Even if he peaks on election day, he'll still lose badly."

Rector Froines shook his head and in a version of his previous gesture, laid his fat man's hand on my knee. Again, it was thoroughly casual and at the same time ugly and ominous, and I understood its gist right away.

"I won't suffer with this any longer, it's too close. Your next move is to get him out of the race, regardless. I don't let politics interfere with business. There's the chance now that someone might pick up on his ideas, whatever they are. I don't take these sorts of risks."

He leaned back in his seat and the car lurched likewise. He didn't look at me.

"It's the only way for everyone," he said, "and it needs to be done now."

I was speechless. Up until now, I had considered Rector Froines to be the lesser of my twin concerns. More threatening overall, perhaps, but also more easily appeased given the certainty of the election's outcome. I tried to reason with him but in the car's stuffy interior, I now felt the full depth and inevitability of the rector's character. His was a predetermined nature, I saw, no more able to refuse rapacity than the earth might resist the sun. In this, I glimpsed for the first time the germ of his religious faith. But before I could capitalize on this observation and get out any words of protest, the rector indicated that it was time for me to leave and Mr. Brunt yanked open the back door. Automatically I pulled myself out of the car and shuffled back inside the grubby eatery. Glancing upward at the diner's sign, I suddenly saw it, too, bore menace toward me. *Where the Customer Always Gets What He Wants*, it read.

Except for a forlorn-looking minister in a beige wash suit, everyone had gone when I returned. However, when he and Trevor looked up to greet me, the man of God saw his opportunity and escaped the table.

"Come to get me, then?" Trevor asked humorously. He stood, not aware, or caring, that his audience had fled him. "And where to now? Are we running late as usual?"

"No, no, we're fine," I said, trying to think of a quiet place and time in the day's itinerary where I could lay out my yet-unconceived arguments for him to quit the campaign. "Wilkie's out back."

I then led him away while he chatted amiably about the issues the ministers and priests and lone rabbi had talked about. One of them, he said, had told a dirty joke about two sisters, a German Shepherd, and a jar of peanut butter. More surprising was that everyone around the table knew the joke and filled in the punchline before he.

He noticed that I was pushing him along to the car.

"We are late," he said sullenly. "I hope it's not to a roundtable or a call-in show. I never get to express myself fully in those situations. The last one you put me on was particularly terrible. Why did they ask me all those questions about food and what I liked to eat? I was tempted to say about how I ate horsemeat as a child. At Grandmama's, on a sandwich with Muenster cheese and butter pickles. I still recall the smell of it. Sweetish and sharp. But it was only that once."

He looked accusingly at me, as if I was to blame for the unpleasant memory.

"It was a cooking show," I said lamely.

We reached Wilkie and got inside the car. Now both he and Trevor looked at me.

"Back to the house," I said, mentally canceling the next campaign stop. "We have a strategy review for eleven."

Satisfied that he was not being taken anywhere against his will, Trevor reclined his front seat and removed his reading glasses, which he then handed to me to keep.

"In that case, I shall rest," he said. "Spiritual exchanges exhaust me, especially with my morning meals. Please don't play any music. I need to sleep now."

XIX

"PEOPLE REALLY ONLY want something when you try to take that something away." This was a saying my bookish and otherwise preoccupied father used to utter when I was small, repeating it whenever I misbehaved and he'd threatened to remove a favorite toy or other plaything. At the time, I wondered if he was saying this to comfort me (telling me in essence that my want for the thing outweighed the thing itself), or to steel himself so he could pursue what he thought was a prudent but difficult course of action. Years later, it occurred to me that he was doing both and was attempting in a concrete moment to pass onto me some of his ambivalent feelings concerning desire and its fulfillment. By then, though, I was already launched into the world of accounting for myself to know firsthand his rueful stance.

Yet because of my understanding of Trevor as someone who responded best on the level of primal interaction, I reflected on this as Wilkie's underpowered car bore us through the morning traffic crawl of Momo-Jima City. In his want of the thing, I thought, Trevor was not much more than a child, though to be fair not many of us evolve that greatly in how we desire. We only learn to tell ourselves that most of what we want is unavailable, silence our needs, and thus call it maturity. Indeed, from infancy to adulthood, I believe the nakedness in our wanting remains the same, despite our ever-growing sophistication in how we avoid confronting this fact.

Still, I felt there was something I could apply of my father's, principle to my situation. At the very least, I knew that trying to convince Trevor to reject the limited success he was now enjoying was not something he could consider, no matter what the circumstances were (I told myself this so I wouldn't dare count on his cooperation, and to anticipate his ready lack of maturity). To jog myself towards a solution then, I performed a mental trick that I've often used to discover a path of action: as an observer might, I viewed myself as another anonymous figure on the landscape, one completely absorbed into his present surroundings and unaware of the larger psychological demands upon his being. This exercise usually had the effect of distancing me from my feelings and clarifying my thoughts.

Thus from the stale sanctuary of the car's backseat, I watched as the stationary world stole by, a low panorama filled with haphazard housing, unreliable-looking restaurants, and customer-free businesses. Now and again, an Asian-style tavern with a French name appeared ("La Poubelle," "Le Ciel Noir") and at the sight of these, I was tempted to tell Wilkie to stop, leave Trevor in the car (where he would drowse for hours if unmolested), and down two or three quick beers to further reflect on myself. I envisioned the cool, wet air of these places, myself in a seat at the deep end of the bar and the low drift of barroom conversation. As we slowly passed them, I felt envy for those so safely lost inside.

Perhaps it was this vision of such unassailable solitude that led me to think of how little use my previous life was in combating my new problem. Seeing myself in sudden relief, almost like a line on a resume, I realized how my background as a reporter had steered me away from dealing with these kinds of dilemmas, given that my professional skills had been used mainly to provoke desires, not restrain them. With every story I wrote, not only did I have to make people want to read more about what I'd covered, but I also needed to convey all the feelings of those I wrote about, as well as the usually disastrous consequences of those emotions. That every other journalist was attempting exactly the same thing did not make me or my colleagues consider alternative methods of reporting; it only increased the competition among us, and the overall clamor of our efforts.

But to kill desire is a far subtler and less resolvable act than to provoke it, and as such, it generally had no place in the meager emotional palette of journalism. Ideally, I'd discovered, the best way to erase that sort of deep feeling was not to stifle it, or even reverse its flow, but to section off that monorail of emotion onto several tributaries of diffuser emotions. In short, it meant introducing doubt as a real notion, as something more than a figment to be conveniently eliminated. Unfortunately, such was usually not possible in journalism since most of it is, above all, innately deterministic, the reader's fifty cents a payment for being convinced that no matter how unreasonable the world, there always is a larger context in which its events might be understood.

Yet as I rode in the back, watching Wilkie's eyes in the rearview mirror as they roved restlessly over the traffic in front of us, I began considering the nature of Trevor's ambition and what other things might quench its strange thirst. I knew he valued the pointless rewards of political power, as well as success in relation to his brother, but was that all? No, I suspected that what he was after was the fearsome quality that separates the merely foolish in politics from the potentially dangerous: the desire for the love of the people (and public service was never more harmed than by any other impulse). He saw himself not in political terms, but unfortunately, in human ones. He was not a legislator so much as a figure—a view I had helped encourage—and thus possessed the tyrant's childish way of nursing immense private hurts in hopes they would be alleviated by the public's eventual recognition that all he wanted was to do it some good. Of course, it was a bad and unforgivable bargain he drove, but acting from rejection was all he knew. Still, in every driven bargain, I thought, there are two players, the actor and the acted-upon and both have the ability to switch places depending on their view of the deal.

Seen this way, I gradually received an explicit signal into my next action, and at the same time, a pang of sorrow for the inert, overgrown form in the front of the car that was now plowing homeward. It was hard to feel otherwise. The child's way, until it proves destructive, is always regrettably easy to sympathize with.

XX

We now sat in the place where we had conducted our first meeting, the narrow shaded porch at the edge of Trevor's backyard. Though he had protested this spot, for psychology's sake I wanted to stay out of the dimly lighted strategy room. Here I felt the open space of the outdoors might reinforce the theme of opportunism I was about to introduce. In this ploy, I recalled and reversed Stalin's infamous unlit vestibule that plunged visitors into sudden darkness just before they met him. Who knows how many bloody deals were consummated after that simple act of intimidation?

Likewise, Trevor's feet once again were planted in his plastic tub of watery balm. That, I noted, was also to my benefit. Immobile, he would be on the receiving end of my physical movements and be forced to consider them without distraction. Still though, he was cross with me, not having recalled the scheduling of a review session and unsure as to what strategy needed to be resolved. He loudly called for the old housemaid and angrily thrust a near-empty pitcher of juice at her to refill before turning his attention to me.

So before he could get too far, I interrupted him.

"Let me speak plainly," I began. "First, I want to commend you. You've done an exceptional job and this campaign has shown you at your finest. The crowds and feeling are genuinely with you and in the eyes of the nation you've proven that you deserve the presidency. That is a tremendous accomplishment considering the many difficulties you've had to overcome. It has been a long but satisfying journey." I paused. "Still, given the circumstances, there's only one alternative available now. It's not easy, but in my opinion, you should quit the race immediately. To preserve your efforts and your good name."

Not used to others having the verbal leap on him, Trevor's mouth worked in silence for a moment. Then his voice discharged in a guttural blast.

"Quit? Are you mad? This is the most support I've ever had! I'm standing now on the verge of triumph!"

I shook my head and replied as smoothly as I could.

"It's the only option left. You've moved among the leaders but that's as high as you'll go. I've just read the most recent polling data from the papers. At this rate, Stanley will win by five to six points, Van Gland will fall away by the weekend, and you'll score another two to three points, maybe four. You're gaining but not quickly enough. The survey is accurate to three percentage points."

"Quit!" He was livid now and rose from his chair, his feet still in the tub. "I am recovering. I am gaining. You said so yourself. What about the newspaper figures?"

"Not fast enough," I repeated. "To win, you need something significant to happen, a dramatic turn or a reversal that can send you in another direction. Barring that, the script is written and will play itself out."

I stopped, then said meaningfully.

"As I said, quitting is your only option."

It was then that he saw I was leading to something and the light came on in his eyes like lamps in a fog bank. He stepped out of his medicine water and padded over to me, sloshing and dripping on the wooden slat floor, his interest in himself pulling him toward his own magnetic north. He gripped my arm tightly.

"My only option?" he asked, hushed. "How?"

"Tomorrow," I answered. "You'll have a press conference surrounded by a crowd of supporters. The subject will ostensibly be your call to increase funding for Esperanto instruction but in a short address, you shall withdraw from the race citing forces that have corrupted the values and leadership you sought to bring to the campaign. Resigning is the only way to maintain your integrity in a crumbling system that continues to deny the will of Momo-Jimans everywhere."

"And where will this leave me?"

"Where you are today. Your name will remain on the ballot since it's too late to remove it and soon it will become known that you don't object to receiving votes as a protest against the current malfeasance in government. After tomorrow, your official campaign is over and you will remain in seclusion until the election. I think we should also come up with a proper name to call your compound since the press is likely to be clustered here for the duration. What about 'Maison Ophelia' after your niece? That way it shows you don't bear Stanley any ill will."

Trevor was unnaturally silent. He stared at me closely before finally speaking.

"It is a good plan, a bloody marvelous one," he said. "I can see why others underestimate you and why I am glad I haven't."

I sighed. Could I never get an unmixed compliment? His comment, meant to please, instead incurred in me a deep notch of irritation since it confirmed what I had long suspected what others' opinions were of me. Even in the midst of praise it is hard to hear that people naturally think less of you. But as they say, others' opinions are merely your own mirrored back (Orozco de Basca—Declaration #11).

"I had better go see about arranging the press conference," I said, politely disengaging myself from his wet grip and trying to keep any resentment out of my voice. "The bigger the crowd tomorrow, the better."

XXI

RECTOR FROINES NATURALLY was pleased when I called to say that Trevor would be resigning. His leaving the race would silence for good all discussion of the mining possibilities on Momo-Jima and now the matter would forever go unmentioned. In response, an hour later, two large baskets of speckled, overly ripe fruit arrived at the hotel. Enclosed was a card that simply read "R. F." though there was no mention of when any payment might be forthcoming.

This time, however, Stanley proved harder to convince of my intentions. It took a long night of argument and two bottles of evil-tasting port before he was able to accept my campaign strategy. I recognized that he was in a peculiar position; though he didn't want to win the election, he didn't wish to lose his legacy, either. That is, he desperately wanted to lose but only to Trevor. In the end, he capitulated to my plan, though I felt he was more convinced not by its possibility for success but by the sure nature of Trevor's defeat if something extraordinary were not attempted.

But as I expected, Trevor's announcement, cloaked as it was in the clinging garment of self-sacrifice, provided another boost to his already forward-moving campaign. Two days after his "quitting," two newspaper surveys showed that Trevor's popularity had climbed an additional half-dozen points, and that the lesser candidates were suffering a rapidly diminishing base of support. It was now a three-man race and Van Gland's fortunes, predicted both papers, figured to be on the wane given his plodding disposition and the more exciting prospect of a brother versus brother showdown.

Indeed, it was this angle more than anything that now vitalized Trevor's candidacy. I saw how right Trevor was in his jailhouse assertion that what the public craved most from its politicians was a good story . . . and here was one properly captivating, biblical in origin. Aiding in this, too, was much fervid coverage by the press in the guise of political analysis. Though such pieces were intricate and preposterous, their effect nevertheless kept the pot of opinion roiling and Trevor's image planted on the front pages. Of all of the aspects of the local media, I thought, this sort of indulgent speciousness harked closest to the American model.

As for me, freed up by the lack of campaigning—per my suggestion, Trevor had secluded himself at Maison Ophelia and granted no interviews—I'd hoped to turn my attention back to Sono. But the new energy of the presidential race had her more engaged than ever, despite one of the candidates having virtually dropped out and the others not communicating anything of substance besides. I phoned and left messages and even stopped by her office twice but was told repeatedly by the cranky-voiced receptionist that Ms. Bando was out and not expected back anytime soon.

Finally, one night as I lay in bed and was about to shut off the reading light, the phone rang. Sono was breathless, as if she'd been out running. I was momentarily alarmed upon hearing her voice. It was high-pitched and urgent and I thought there might be some sort of immediate emergency.

"Ah, good. I've caught you," she said.

"Sono?"

"Of course. Who were you expecting?"

"No one. But I've been phoning."

"I know. I've gotten the messages. Sweet of you to leave so many. Or perhaps I should be menaced by your persistence."

She laughed and I saw that nothing was wrong. She was simply still full of the exhilarated campaign temperament that I'd had up until a few days ago. But whereas I'd gotten off the train, so to speak, she was on board to the trip's end. I would be at the terminus, too, but my temporary departure had quelled me enough to leave me to some thoughts of my own invention.

At any rate, her words flowed and she spoke quickly.

"What are you doing?" she asked.

"Doing? Nothing . . . reading." For some reason, I was reluctant to tell her I was in bed, ready to fall asleep a good deal before midnight.

"I've just finished my stories for tomorrow. A long one on the landowners' view of the candidates and a short wrap of the day's events. You know Bergeron quit this afternoon, don't you?"

"I've heard. Not that surprising, considering."

In truth, this development came as news but again I hesitated to reveal my true state of things to Sono. I was keenly aware that in just five days away from active participation, I was already out of the push and tangle of these clamorous events. Mainly, my job now consisted of trying to deflect overt press scrutiny while at the same time quietly spreading the word that Trevor would welcome all public support at the polls. For the latter, I'd contacted a number of his more ardent supporters, supplied them with boxes of signs, stickers, and banners, as well as the phone numbers and addresses of registered voters, and instructed them to do whatever they needed to firm up the ranks of sympathizers who might be discouraged from voting.

Beyond that, however, my role had officially ceased to exist. The tizziness I'd felt from my involvement in the campaign lasted only as long as such media-induced tizziness usually does, which is to say it was over almost as soon as I'd stepped off the train.

"I've just finished interviewing him," she said. "He's thinking of giving his support to Trevor."

"I wish he'd reconsider," I answered. "It wasn't that much to begin with and he's a prime headache to deal with. Trying to schedule a TV debate with him was impossible."

"Still it counts for something. He's strong with the retirees, the first-generation folks. They believe he isn't going to squander their leisure benefits. They'll be sorry he's gone."

I let her last remark hang, unwilling to enter into any more discussion of the current raging trivia.

"So," she said again, "what're you doing?"

"Actually, I'm in bed. Almost sleeping." It was my turn to laugh. "What did you have in mind?"

"A drink maybe? I'm too awakened to sleep and I don't want to go back to Nao's. Half the kids are sick and the two of them are fighting. I'll be up all night."

"A drink, then. Where shall we go?"

"I'll come over to you. I took some bottles of champagne from Bergeron's office while they were clearing out. Everyone was looting so it seemed right to follow along. Are you surprised at me? It's good champagne."

"I'm more surprised they bought the bottles. They couldn't have been expecting a celebration."

"I'll meet you in the lobby. We'll go for a drive. I've just bought myself a car and I need to practice."

"You've got a new car?"

"Surprised now? It's old but it's sturdy. Maybe you can give me some pointers on driving."

"Don't you have a license?"

"Don't be silly. You can't apply for one unless you've got a car."

"I've never heard of anything like that."

"It makes perfect sense. I've never heard of anything else. Why else would one want to learn?"

"But aren't there a lot of accidents, especially at night? What about teenagers? Isn't anyone concerned about their driving?"

"There're some crashes I imagine, . . . look, do you want to go for a drink or not?"

"But what's open at this time?"

I was determined, it seemed, to make things hard for myself.

"How should I know what's open now?" she said with exasperation. "I'm a working girl. I'm at home in bed most nights."

XXII

A half hour later, Sono drove up in a gleaming brown Oldsmobile, roaring and gunning through the humid night air. It was the old car I'd seen on the lawn of Stanley's house, still without license plates but now fixed up to drive and pulsing along with a loud, bottom-heavy shudder. From across the parking lot, I saw that its whitewall tires were large and new, as were the silver rims, and the tail and sidelights glowed ferociously in the dark. Getting in, I felt its concentrated heat blast me from the powerful engine. It was a remarkable, animalistic thing and it struck me as incongruous that a nervous, frangible presence such as Stanley's would own it, much less drive it.

"It's mine now," Sono said pridefully as we drove off. "This used to be Stanley's official car, along with a driver, but he wanted a cheaper one so he could sell this and cash in the difference. Only no one bought it for what he was asking and he got stuck footing the bill for a brand–new government vehicle. I negotiated and gave him half down with the rest coming. I'll own it outright in a month."

Sono grinned at my surprise at her. As the car passed under a row of streetlights, I could see that she had come straight from work and had time to make only minimal changes to herself. Over her linen office ensemble, she had thrown a black suede jacket, thin and shiny with age, and she'd also untied her dark hair to go loose to her shoulders. The accumulated odors of an indoors work day, along with the scent of menthol cigarettes, also clung faintly to her.

To mask them, she'd applied a fresh coat of a heavy, fragrant perfume. A gardenia-like scent that filled the car as we drove.

"I've always wanted an old car like this," she said enthusiastically, "even with all the trouble of keeping it up. I saw an old Chevelle the other day being loaded on a freighter to Pakistan. I guess the owner was taking it with him. How he'll manage it there, I don't know."

She motioned with her head toward the back. "The champagne's on the floor. It's supposed to be good. I'll let you tell me."

I reached around behind me and found a grocery bag containing several bottles of Blanc de Blanc, two plastic wine goblets, and some torn-off labels that read, "President Bergeron's Reserve." Examining a bottle by the light of the glove box, I saw it was a costly vintage. I recognized it from a Hollywood human rights function that I had once covered but had not been permitted to eat or drink at.

"It's fine," I said. "Expensive, in fact."

"It should be. Bergeron is privately wealthy. His family owns a swarm of medical supply and prostheses shops throughout Southeast Asia. Quite lucrative after the wars. Surely you've seen the ads: 'Why Pay an Arm and a Leg for an Arm and a Leg?' Give me a glass."

I carefully removed the cork from a bottle and held the champagne near the floor to not wet the seats and I poured a small glass. The liquid bubbled and trembled but did not foam over. Sono took the goblet and drank it meditatively.

"Chilled, it'd be better." She then held out her goblet for a refill as she concentrated on the darkened highway in front of us. Though the road was straight and she drove only moderately fast, my anxiety over her nascent ability, coupled with my natural trepidation over night travel, made me grateful that there were few other vehicles on the road. Mostly, there were just slow-moving trucks taking up the interior lanes with their lumbering ways. We came upon them suddenly, their fuzzy orange lights blinking fitfully in the dark and then in a second or two disappearing fastly behind us. We drank awhile in the rumble and quiet, and slowly I felt my nerves ease up.

"So," Sono asked after a few moments, "where shall we go?" She looked at me sidelong. "Is there somewhere you haven't been? A place still left on your tourist's agenda?"

I shrugged. "Not likely. I think I've seen everything here to see." But then remembering my earlier comments, I stopped myself.

"Just like a reporter. I know it's hard not to know everything."

"Ex-reporter," I said pointedly, as much to myself as to her.

She drove on for a few moments, thinking.

"Well, I do know a spot on the north end," she said. "It's not in any of the guidebooks. But it's reasonably lit and there's music and food, if you're hungry. But you don't look like you need any propping up."

She gave me a sly look. "Do you?"

Swiftly, she braked to a stop on the road's soft shoulder and turned the car around in the opposite direction.

I said nothing. Under the glow of the champagne, the accelerating car, and Sono's command of direction, I found I was becoming mesmerized by the darkness into which we were driving. It was an island blackness that seemingly arose from the vast surrounding ocean to absorb all of the radiant light and sink it back miles deep into the quiet sea. The hypnotic, throaty pulsation of the car's engine added to the overall sense of unreality. At any moment, I almost expected the ground to fall away and for us to begin levitating through the upper exosphere which, like the flapping waters below, would be swathed in a great tomb of silence.

"It's beautiful at night," said Sono, partially reading my thoughts. "And desolate, too, though I suppose that's what makes it appealing."

"A poet once wrote that night is our natural home outside of the world," I responded, "and that we enter and leave it each time at our peril."

I glanced at her, slightly embarrassed.

"But I've never been clear whether he meant the greater danger was in coming or going. Or maybe it's the journey back and forth."

Sono looked at me sidelong again, this time more skeptically.

"Never mind that, what about your real home? Don't you miss it? Haven't you been here a month already?"

"Just three weeks," I said, annoyed that my thoughts had been so abruptly grounded back to the mundane. "About twice as long as I'd planned. But you're right. No matter how well you get along in a place, there's always something that makes you feel lonely about being away."

"I can't imagine you'd had time for loneliness. Since when have you been by yourself?"

"It's not just about being by yourself," I said, "it's about the times you get tired of always being responsible for your feelings. Usually on a long trip, there's always one moment when everything you do and every place you can go seems pointless and all the new things around you just drive you back into yourself. You walk down the streets thinking about what led you to be where you are, right here at this point in time, and hoping at every corner and door slam to meet someone who'll take you out of yourself, even for just a few hours. That's when the country seems too big a place and all you want is to have a private corner of it with nothing to think about."

I emptied the remainder of the bottle into my toy-like goblet.

"But that usually doesn't happen more than once and I've already had my moment."

I put away the bottle and waited for Sono to respond but instead she was slowing the car and peering at the road, hunting for a direction. A stone-pocked metal sign and a gravel road materialized along the berm and she hunched forward, looking closer.

"I think we're here," she said.

She turned up the path and navigated slowly on the bumpy trail, stopping the car after a few hundred feet as the road became a natural pier that extended into the ocean. I was surprised that we had arrived so quickly and I laid aside my glass and gazed ahead into the murk.

But as my eyes adjusted to this even deeper pitch of night, what I saw in front of us was exactly what I had sought earlier while driving with Wilkie and what I had imagined back home: a view that allowed the entirety of one's vision to be encompassed by water. No land or human references, just the ocean expanse, admonishing, it seems, all that we suffer and dream up being exiled on solid ground.

Gazing at it, I realized this vision had also been visiting me in my last moments before I fell asleep at night.

I rolled down the window and the ocean's wet air entered the car. I breathed deeply to fill my lungs as much as possible. A part of me was moved by a growing feeling of exhilaration.

"All right, then," Sono said, cutting the engine and flicking off the headlights. "Let's drink the champagne and enjoy the view. And enough talk of loneliness."

I watched the dark ocean rise and collapse a few more moments, its phosphorescence fitfully sparking out on the sand below.

"I'm not lonely now," I said.

I turned to Sono, then instinctively pulled her toward me. There was a delicious, inconclusive stop before we tumbled forth and kissed once, then again twice more.

"Let me get rid of my glass," she said.

She pulled away, dropped her empty goblet on the floor, and moved back to me. Her lips, hair, skin, and gardenia scent came together in an indistinct tangle, with the snap of the champagne rising above it. Under her clothes, I felt her body press and twist and sink against mine as we embraced; again, the overwhelming sensation I had was of moving deeper and deeper inside an overall darkness in which my movements were now weightless and unbound.

After several minutes, she broke away again and put a hand on my face. It was a light, birdlike gesture, one of rest rather than retreat, and her voice when she spoke was breathless.

"If you don't mind, the backseat's a lot more comfortable," she said thickly. "These old cars give you lots and lots of room."

XXIII

MUCH LATER, WHILE recalling the passage of the next few days, I found that I remembered everything about them in exacting detail. This was greatly unlike me and it presented a problem that I'd never before encountered—that of trying to analyze events without knowing their individual impact upon me. Usually, my memory is acutely selective, consisting of heightened experiences, which by their impact have helped me to understand them. But to remember things in toto, especially during such a disordered time, has made it impossible to sort through the tumult of those days to establish their precise character, which even now remains a mystery to me.

What I can do is simply relate the events as they ensued.

Following my night (and subsequent early morning) with Sono, I was reluctantly thrown back into the campaign. Though I would have liked to linger with her, pleasurably ignorant of time, the next day was election eve and the respite I'd enjoyed from Trevor's abjuration was to be replaced either by managing the attention of the press if he proved victorious, or by plying enough succor and wiles on Trevor to ease my situation if he lost. That Sono also had to become similarly busy made it only slightly easier.

Most immediately, though, I had many tedious campaign duties to attend to. The entire day before the election I traversed the length and breadth of the island with Wilkie to reassure supporters in every precinct that voting for Trevor would be a purposeful act, not just fatuous rebellion. It was an interminable day. We began our trek shortly after eight in the morning, took no breaks, and I was not back at the hotel until midnight. By the end, I was completely wrung out and sweaty from hours of human contact. In the hotel lobby, I purchased my dinner from the bank of vending machines and had no thoughts other than of getting out of my clothes and opening the last bottle of champagne that had been leftover from my evening with Sono.

But later that night, Trevor phoned. His voice was unlike any I had ever heard—an unsettling mix of desperation and jocularity, accompanied by the peculiar insistence that we meet at once. But though it was past two a.m. and I should have been sleeping since I had an early morning media appointment (now just a few hours away), I was similarly anxious and restlessly watching the diminishing channels on television. For that reason, I did not object too hard when he pressed me. On election eve, I thought, all bets were bound to be off. Poor Wilkie then came to fetch me, looking exactly as he did all day. His only concession to the hour was to play his opera tapes extra loudly, perhaps to keep himself awake.

Trevor was waiting in the strategy room when I let myself in his airless house thirty minutes later. Given the hour, he was dressed oddly, as if he expected to be leaving for an imminent appointment. Under a new gray suit, he wore a green button-down shirt and a fashionable, tongue-colored tie. His coat was fully buttoned and he had on formal black shoes that made heavy sounds on the wooden floor as he walked. Only the slight tremble and wobble in his posture, a sign he had been drinking, indicated that he would likely be staying in for the night.

Still, as I entered, he uttered no greeting and gave no acknowledgement that I had arrived, other than a slight quizzical nod. Instead, he kept staring intently at a small keepsake on his bookshelf. With a shudder, I recognized the object as a fist-sized piece of amber in which a silver, multi-tentacled insect had been trapped many thousands of years ago. I had picked it up before, found it repellent, and put it away. Now, though, Trevor scrutinized it as though he expected the ephemera to suddenly become animated in his presence. I stood waiting for several moments for a signal of greater recognition from him, then gave up and sat down. I estimated I waited in the dimly lit room for approximately ten minutes before he finally spoke.

"Soon it will be over," said Trevor heavily, turning away from his off-putting memento to face me. "Done, done. Everything all done."

I was glad he could not clearly see my reaction in the darkened room, either to the fossil or now to his absurd manner. To me, his voice rang like a third-rate actor's auditioning for the part of a haunted spirit. Even for him, it verged on the unbelievable.

"You realize that now, don't you?" he continued. "I have only recently come to accept it as fact."

Naturally, I had no idea what he was talking about so instead I concentrated harder on the timbre of his voice. Beneath its silly resonance, I judged it to be sadder and more desolate than it had been over the phone.

"It's hard to understand, this long progression that's meant to add up to something," he went on. "Every new moment promising what the old one withholds, and our obediently playing along with the conceit. Until we come to the end of the string and discover that it's all been a purposeless tangle and that like children we expected it to have an apparent conclusion. Then what do we propose to do?"

On his desk I saw an opened bottle of something medicinal-looking, though I could not tell through the brown barrel how much of it had been used. But as Trevor noticed my gaze, he quickly limped over to cap the bottle.

"Nerve restorative," he said curtly.

He shoved the bottle into a drawer, then turned to face me.

"Ben, I have come to the end of my string prematurely and I need help."

His addressing me by name startled me. I realized I had unconsciously adopted the pose of an audience and had not expected to be spoken to. Perhaps I, too, had come to view him more as a suitable fiction than as a living being.

"What is it?" I asked. "Did something happen?"

Instead of answering me directly, he shook his head and crossed the room to his desk. Standing behind it, he switched on a small desk lamp that bathed him in a harsh and unflattering glow. He then took up his drink and began speaking again as if I had faded back beyond the footlights.

"Tomorrow will decide how I spend the next three years, whether in permanent retirement here or in public exile as a head of state," he said. "I now have a good idea that I might win. I've read the polling data you've collected. It couldn't have been from the regular sources, it's too good. Where did you get it?"

Because it had been gotten illicitly from Sono, I mumbled something low and vague, hoping he would let it pass. For a moment, he held out for an answer, then went on.

"Doesn't matter. The issue I need advice on refers to my own private terrors. Never have I been more afraid in my life."

"Of what?"

"Bad things," he muttered. "Incomprehensible almost." He looked up with a black expression on his face, the unhinged effect of which was enhanced by the electric glare that overlit him.

"Do you know the feeling of sitting on the perch of victory?" he asked in a voice filled with dread. "You must. You've experienced good fortunes. You know the whip of success . . . you probably are accustomed to it. But all of this is foreign to me. I've never succeeded in anything before. My life has been a continual parade of defeats, some slim and some overwhelming, but losses all the same. I know losing as well as some men know their wives after decades of marriage. Perhaps losing has been my main companion and why I have stayed alone."

I was about to say something but thought better of it and let him go on.

"Even as a boy, I rarely had victories. In sports, or among the grown-ups, or at school, Stanley continually made the greater impression. The things I tried, he always bested me at. For example, I remember playing billiards as a teenager. I would play for hours just for the love of it. Then I conceived it as a way to triumph over Stanley and I devoted even more time to it. Yet one summer when we were both home from our universities, he took me on and beat me in rotation pool, game after game. It was the first truly crushing moment of my life. I'd suffered losses before but I'd always told myself that tomorrow would bring triumph if I could manage to persevere. But from that day, I began to believe in the permanence of my own failure. From then on, I felt my pattern was indelibly set. I was just twenty. That he was younger made it all the worse."

He stopped to sip his drink.

"And naturally, his success in one event lent him the confidence to develop other abilities. People never speak of how easy it is to reap achievements in other areas once you've become acquainted with victory, but it's true. I've since watched him climb from success to success. For myself, it has been the opposite. Until now, I have only one real achievement I can claim and find solace in."

"What is it?" I asked, instantly curious about this human aspect of him.

Trevor paused, hesitant. His element of modesty was new to me.

"Mind you, it's not a great exploit but it is a talent I have developed and it is mine alone."

"Of course."

I nodded by way of inducement before softening my voice in sympathy.

"Please," I said. "I'd like to know."

"Well," he said slowly, "I do impersonations . . . of world leaders. It's practically my full-time hobby. I study their photographs and videos, and if possible, listen to their speeches and read their biographies. In the past, I've successfully attempted Marcos, de Gaulle, Suharto, even Franco and Chiang Kai-shek. In their native tongues, too, though naturally I'm better with the English-speaking ones."

He brightened.

"Do you want to see my Margaret Thatcher?"

"Perhaps later," I suggested quickly.

"No, of course not. Silly." He gulped the rest of his glass and returned to the subject.

"Let me put it plain then. What I have always relied on for my identity in life has been the surety of defeat. It has been a steady and reliable provider, and after I learned to accept its presence, I've had no complaints. But to succeed now means undertaking a new personality with new thoughts, motivations and responsibilities. I am nearing sixty years old. How can I expect to fulfill this? Who will I become and how? And what will they ..."—here he indicated outwards to the greater public—"... expect to see in me?"

He looked at me sadly.

"It may strike you as fraudulent but each time I have run, I never expected to win. I always put forth the effort knowing that it was a futile piece of work. Some would say that this is a mark of my character, the refusal to be beaten down by odds. I wonder instead if these efforts have simply made me a higher grade form of liar."

He paused and said in a trembling voice, "For that is how I would describe myself."

I felt he was on the verge of openly weeping and I very nearly made a move to comfort him. But I also felt this would be fraudulent on my part. Trevor had always stood at a distance from me (engaging me, of course, under frank coercion) and now it seemed that this display, too, as heartfelt as it seemed, was simply more reinforcement of the superior's prerogative to take out his emotions on a subordinate.

At any rate, I stayed in my chair and gradually he composed himself.

"Not everyone is prepared to assume what they've been given," I offered gently when he stopped. "Most have to adapt to their new roles. Maybe you'll be invigorated by it. Look at the number of writers who found their voice late in life or the artists who came upon their talents in retirement. It is never too late to start over."

I said this last sentence with my tongue high in my mouth to keep an even tone and not betray my own disbelief. Usually, the gift of a late renaissance is extremely rare. For too many people, the opportunity to begin again and again only grounds them in intense purposelessness since they never absorb the weight of permanent loss. To repeatedly start over with undiluted enthusiasm, and scale, is akin to a child's passion for his newest mail-order toy.

I also could not think of any examples of well-known late-blooming artists, or at least any I'd liked.

"Some people would consider you fortunate," I went on. "Not only haven't you suffered from too-early success, but you've also gained perspective on how to judge your triumph. Now you'll regard your victory in its proper light and won't succumb from it. That's of enormous value. Isn't that the primary lesson of history? That we are never as vulnerable as after our greatest successes?"

Although Trevor still refused to acknowledge them, I saw my words had made some progress. By way of response, he now began to maunder about the murky, cluttered room, his limp having disappeared. Stopping by a long shelf of photographs of himself, he slowly examined them one by one, picking them up and setting them down after intense scrutiny. Some of the images were quite old, dating back to college, while others appeared to have been snapped just recently. In nearly all of them, he was posed alone.

"I wonder why it is we take so many pictures of ourselves," he said solemnly. "After a certain point, it seems their only purpose is to record our decline, not the fullness of our lives. For the emotions they evoke are never happy ones. If the occasion was a good one, we're sad that it's passed. If the experience was unhappy, then we recall the misery of that moment. Do you have any happy photographs of yourself?"

I replied negligibly for something in his manner had distracted me into a deeper reflection. His way with the pictures reminded me of an elephant sniffing at the bones of his fallen comrades. "All these remains and there is nothing that survives," I imagined the animal lamenting. But in Trevor's case, the mourning seemed to be directed at himself for himself.

I sat up in my chair and put down my drink, having acquired an insight into his feeling. It triggered a minor flutter of sympathy and a larger one of recognition.

"If I can speak frankly, I think I know why you feel the way you do," I said.

Trevor turned quizzically toward me, his mouth slightly open. Every time he laughed, his face bore the original source of little boy humor that'd fueled his sense of amusement for life. And every time he winced there was the nature of the first pain. I could see him now girding for the latter.

"You don't fear victory," I went on, "you only fear the attention it brings. What makes losing comfortable for you is its anonymity. Because a contest can have dozens, even hundreds of losers, it's easy to say, 'I tried and I lost,' since that's what everyone expects. But when there is a winner, he becomes the object of others' attention. Suddenly, he has admirers who want to be like him, but more importantly, he also has enemies who wish to be in his place. And for those who don't know the circumstances of true friendship, it must be unbearable to think of the people who, for no reason, now dislike you."

I paused as he took his eyes off me and looked away.

"You've never had that many friends but now that you're about to succeed, you stand to only make enemies," I said. "Left unrecognized, you would have never known of them and their feelings toward you. But winning will expose you to them."

My words visibly pierced him and for a moment I feared that he would physically collapse. The imagined rebuke of strangers, more stinging at times than the worst censures from intimates, I thought. But he merely sagged a little and then began speaking in a hushed, faraway–sounding voice that seemed not to refer to himself but instead to someone else's unmentionable misfortune.

"You're very keen," he said. "Companionship is a gift that always has eluded me, even to my age. I have never been happier than in these last few weeks with all those who are supporting me. The crowds have been beyond my imagining. It is the affection that every public figure wishes for deep in his heart. But now my supporters will likely turn into my adversaries. I could not have invented this kind of irony, nor do I know now how to escape it."

"But you've no choice, you've come too far," I responded. "Maybe before they might have dismissed you but this time there is a strong feeling for you. Now they'll resent you if you don't live up to the moment. You've made an overture to them and this is what they expect."

I stood and crossed the room until I was next to him.

"One doesn't come by friendship if they're unwilling to risk enemies," I said. "It's the natural way of things. To choose some is to naturally reject others. Either way, there's no going back. You can't think there is."

"I have never been without acquaintances," he said manfully, struggling to regain a touch of his pride. "Women friends, too, on rare occasion. But they've all disappeared, though I don't know how. God knows what they must think of me, if they ever do."

He turned to me and I could see wetness in his eyes. Here was the hopeful boy left alone on the playground, I thought, waiting for someone to come back to play with him but knowing that he'd likely been deserted again.

"Yet I reflect on them quite often," he said.

"You mustn't think that way," I replied, putting a hand on his shoulder and drawing my analysis and comfort to a close. "It's no crime to be friendless, it's only sad. And soon now, it will be over."

XXIV

I BEGAN THE next day a few hours later in the aseptic setting of an old-fashioned television studio where I was being interviewed. Like the US, Momo-Jima had been beset by a proliferation of morning question-and-chat shows (three apiece on each of its three channels) and I was scheduled to be on two of them today. A few other candidates and their handlers were also to appear but since Trevor was considered the primary story of the election, and since he had refused to make any public appearances for several days, my presence was of the highest priority and I led off the panel of guests on both shows.

For twenty minutes then, and against a panoramic backdrop of a flock of Guanche birds rising off the early morning waters, I was battered with unanswerable questions asked in the disjointed manner of conversational television. Keeping my part of the bargain, I said absolutely nothing of substance in return, and for this, I was thanked profusely and escorted by a driver (poor Wilkie had finally been given the day off) to a rival channel so I could repeat myself. As I left this first show, I passed several guests waiting to follow me, among them the white-mustached man I'd seen a few weeks earlier on the soap opera. He was helping himself to liberal portions from the morning buffet and shards of cheese, ham, and croissants had become stuck in the heavy brush of his whiskers. As he talked animatedly with the other guests, these crumbs fell to the floor in a circle around him.

The second show took longer than the first, which is to say that the guest slated to follow me ran late and forced me to stay on the air an extra fifteen minutes enduring additional conversation. Still, like my first appearance, I resolutely gave out no information, nor said anything of value, conduct for which again I was rewarded with gratitude and this time a gift certificate to a car rental agency on the island. From there I was driven back. By the time my amiable driver (who knew nothing of the election, of Trevor, or of government matters in general, only of European football) dropped me off at Maison Ophelia, it was nearly nine a.m.

Despite the early hour, there was a knot of reporters already camped out on Trevor's wet and scrubby front lawn. I looked for Sono, then recalled her telling me that she was to be roving among the candidates that day, the paper's only other staffer having come down with a well-timed case of the shingles. Seeing the press, I told the driver to use the driveway onto the property. I then got out at the end and hurried through the back door into the house.

From the stillness inside, I understood Trevor to be asleep. To my dismay, however, I also saw Wilkie reclining in the living room. He evidently did not have the day off. I took him aside.

"When did you arrive?" I asked him.

"Around five, I think," he replied.

"Did he call you to come back?"

"She did," he said, meaning the housekeeper. "I think she wanted a man around in case he got into something."

I nodded and left him alone to rest. More and more, my admiration for Wilkie, already substantial by now, swelled. Not only did he have an unshakable equanimity in every situation I'd seen him, but he also had the rare trait of containing his feelings so they would not interrupt the natural flow of others' conduct. In this way, he brought out people's true essence (a born reporter, I thought).

Still, despite his refusal to impose on others, his own feelings themselves were deep and complex. You could see some of this in the way he listened to his opera. It was not just a music lover's rapture but rather the experience of someone who simultaneously appreciated, critiqued, and accepted the destiny of the sound and the choices made in the passages. He was at once the listener, composer, and aesthetician. I had never met anyone like him.

Now, though, he was worn out and gray-looking. He sunk himself down in an overstuffed chair and soon I heard the deep ligamental rhythms of his hard sleep.

The housekeeper (I learned her name was Mrs. Mowry) wasn't to be seen as I padded through the rest of the quiet house. Entering the strategy room, I came upon the remains of the night before: the empty bottle of nerve tonic, some cigars Trevor apparently had smoked after I left, and his formal black shoes, which were left by the door. Mrs. Mowry evidently wasn't that scrupulous a housekeeper or else she didn't come in here unless Trevor was present. I opened a window to let out the stale air, glancing at all the poor reporters stranded on the lawn and who would be there for many hours to come, and leaned back for a moment on the green velour sofa. It was plush and yielding and the air that entered through the window was cool and fresh. . . .

I next recall being shaken awake by the insistent tremor of Wilkie's meaty hands. The sun now shone in my eyes, hurting them, and judging by the position of it in the room, it was probably around noon.

"Mr. Inoue, there's someone on the phone," he said. "She says she needs to speak with you."

I struggled up and looked at my watch. It was a good deal past noon, nearly one-thirty, and my bones ached from the spongy support of the couch. I also realized a cotton blanket had been thrown over me and that my shoes had been taken off. My mouth was very dry.

"Who is it?" I asked.

"She didn't say," said Wilkie, already leading me out of the room. "Just asked for you in a hurry."

I stopped to put on my shoes and followed after Wilkie, who was now in the kitchen and holding the phone for me. He handed it over and left. Sono spoke to me from the other end.

"Hello to you," she said. "They told me you were sleeping but I said to wake you up. I hope you don't mind."

I filled a short glass with water from the tap and drank it down—tasting the rust in it too late—before answering.

"Where are you?" I asked.

"Just leaving Moatley's. On my way to Stanley's to watch him vote. It's already been a long day."

"Are you coming here? We can get lunch."

"Had it an hour ago. Besides, I'm working and I don't mix business and play. But I have a good story to tell you."

"You've mixed them before. I recall you liking it then."

"Stop. Do you want to hear or not?"

"All right, tell me."

Suddenly there was a noisy siren blast on her end and we were momentarily interrupted.

"Sorry, an air horn just went off," she said after the noise stopped. "They're trying to rally the troops, though God knows why. Can you hear me?"

"Go ahead."

"It's about Moatley's pollsters," she began, not hearing my reply and shouting occasionally to be heard above the din. "You know about them, don't you? The ones doing the exit surveys? He hired a few dozen of them. Teenagers mostly, for a few hours at sub-minimum wages. From the Izumi precinct down to Nakada. The thinking was that if the numbers are tight, there's enough time to make a late campaign swing in the afternoon. And the surveys will tell him where to go."

"Sounds logical," I answered. "And economical."

"Well, about two hours ago, they called in their first totals," she continued, still not listening to me. "You should have been here, the place went mad. Absolutely loony. Apparently, Moatley had gotten a terrific number of votes. Around a thousand and it wasn't even noon yet. When the second round came in, it was even better. According to the pollsters, he had about three thousand votes."

"That would seem to be the election," I said.

"Of course it was," she said. "Everyone here thought so. So fifteen minutes later, they gathered us around for a press conference and start handing out releases saying that Oswaldo Moatley had pulled off 'the most tremendous Election Day miracle in modern political history.' That's straight from the script with more pompous hogwash from there. But just as Moatley gets up and starts going on about how the voting's not over but here are his plans for the country, anyway, in case anyone's interested, an aide pushes his way through and hustles him off and the press conference's over. Later, a volunteer came back and we found out what really happened. It turned out that all the pollster kids were bought off by Van Gland's people to call in fake totals. Their thinking was that if Moatley thought he had big numbers, he wouldn't go out campaigning. So the kids began piling on the numbers, spreading them around several precincts, but still making it look like a huge win for Moatley. In reality, though, they had a hard time finding anyone who'd admitted to voting for him. They think now that Moatley's got about six hundred votes, total. Someone came around later and literally snatched the releases out of our hands, though I managed to keep one."

Another blast erupted on the other end, separating us again for several seconds before she resumed.

"What a screwup," said Sono with the journalist's unadorned glee at a good story arising from the misfortune of others. "I saw Moatley later. He looked completely destroyed. He thought this was going to be the best day of his life. Everyone's trying to get to the manager—he's the one who screwed the pollsters to start with—but he's nowhere around."

She broke off to yell something at someone and returned.

"I'm writing it now but I don't know how much of it I can tell. Moatley knows the publisher's son and might get it killed. But if we don't run it, the *Avoucher* or the *Edifier* will." She sighed and let the futility of occupational hazards hover in the air for a moment.

"So how's it on your end?" she continued. "Anything good to tell me?"

"Nothing that good," I said. "Actually, it's very quiet here. I haven't seen Trevor all morning and I haven't even looked at my messages. You're the first person I've talked to. Maybe I can ask you about the exit polls."

"Haven't got our numbers but we'll be getting some in about an hour. I'll call you then or maybe I'll stop by."

"Work or play?"

"Don't split hairs," she said and hung up.

On my own again, I went to find Trevor. I ventured first into the living room but it was still dark and empty. I then went to the rear of the house but he was not in his bedroom, either. Guessing that he would not be in the strategy room since it was so recently occupied by me, I was about to go into the backyard when I encountered Mrs. Mowry, who was carrying several men's suits sheathed in dry cleaner's wrap.

"He went out driving with Mr. Wilkie and that naked man just after you woke up," she said tersely. "Wait a second."

She handed me the suits, then reached deep into the pockets of her baggy sweatsuit for a notepad. She tore off the top several sheets and we exchanged the pages for the dry cleaning.

"Here're your messages. They've been calling all morning. The reporters outside have been waiting to talk to you, too. One of them even walked into the room while you were sleeping. Mr. Wilkie threw him out."

Thanking her as she left, I stood in the hallway and ran through my calls. I saw to my relief that only a few of them could be acted upon. Most were last-minute requests from supporters for campaign help or materials (and in one case, money) that were impossible to attend to now. There were also several calls from the press (these I put away) and a message apiece from Stanley and Rector Froines. I ducked into the bathroom for a leisurely wash-up, then went back into the kitchen to use the phone, debating who I should talk to first.

But just as I took hold of the receiver to make my first call, the phone rang in my hand. Over a terrible racket, the welcome voice of Wilkie began shouting into my ear. Through the noise, I had difficulty making him out.

"I think you'd better get here," I finally heard him say. "There's been trouble."

"Trouble? Where are you?"

"What?"

"Where are you?" I shouted, a bellow that brought the scowling Mrs. Mowry immediately into, and then out of, the kitchen.

"Grande Place," Wilkie shouted back. "He's been arrested. Turn on the radio. It's . . ."

There was an extra-loud burst of tumult on the other end and then the line was snatched away and went dead.

I held the receiver, stunned. Arrested? Now what? For the first time in several days, I felt the familiar, sickening charge of confusing and overpowering events wash over me. In my absence from the campaign, I'd lost touch with this wayward slam but now it was back. For a long moment I simply considered my situation, damning myself that I now had knowledge that required acting upon. Then reluctantly but mechanically I reached for a notebook and pen, and checked myself for my watch, money, passport, and keys. As I left the kitchen, I shouted to Mrs. Mowry to wait for my call.

Exiting cautiously from the rear of the house to avoid the reporters in front, I found to my surprise that none now remained on the lawn. Evidently, they'd all been pulled into whatever events were transpiring at the plaza. This was not a good sign, I thought. What could be so encompassing as to command the attention of every last one of them? Walking more quickly, I turned down the empty street to search for a taxi. But the unnatural stillness of the national holiday—Election Day—had settled on the neighborhood and I could find few signs of commerce, transportation, or sidewalk traffic. Even the dogs were inside.

Jogging now, and with a growing rise of desperation, I passed through several more unsuccessful blocks. But each one seemed quieter than the next as though I was heading away from the epicenter of activity. Had I not known of the holiday, I might have thought that all the city's residents had been evacuated in the face of a pending natural disaster or had been locked away due to an epidemic. There was only a solitary patrolman who regarded me suspiciously as I went running past him on his slow-pedaling bicycle.

I was about to reverse my course when suddenly I came upon an unattended taxi parked outside a morose-looking storefront chapel.

Painted in ominous gray and black stripes, the church ("Les Yeux de Lourdes") seemed more like a monument to self-flagellation than to spiritual inspiration. Echoing this was its overhead frieze that showed a crippled man clutching at an angel who was clearly ambivalent over his petition. Still, given the collective closure of the surrounding area, I headed toward it like a dog to a long-lost owner. I paused a moment at the entrance to wipe my face, then pushed open the door.

Inside, the sacellum was cool and empty except for a middle-aged man locked in prayer at the large plastic altar. Beside him was a broken fountain and a set of well-worn purple knee benches that fronted the artificial Jesus. These, however, were the only signs that this was a place of worship; otherwise, the room's spirit and anonymous decor reminded me more of a company break area. As the man didn't look up when I entered, I took a seat in the back row of metal folding chairs to wait for him to finish communing. But then, thinking better of it, I went into the men's room where I cooled my face with wet paper towels.

When I returned, the man was still supplicating, though now in a much quicker rhythm. Clearly, from his urgency he had a great deal to ask for. Still, the press of other events was weighing on me. In what I considered to be a cheery but efficient manner I stood and addressed him.

"Excuse me, but isn't that your taxi outside?"

The man gave no response and continued his rapid mumblings. I angled a few steps closer so he might see me from his peripheral vision.

"I'm sorry for interrupting but it's important. Is that your cab outside?"

Without taking himself out of his position, the man halted his prayers and turned his face toward me. It was a queer countenance, milky white with several reddish melanin patches, as if drops of dark paint had been dripped on him at birth. His eyes were deep and narrow and above them he seemed to have only the thinnest of eyebrows; looking at them, I was reminded of the woman's practice of plucking the brows and then filling them in with pencil. Conversely, the lower half of his face was fitted with a rugged jaw and wide-set mouth that worked slowly as he spoke.

"Please," he said mournfully, "leave me alone. I am praying for my sister's gall bladder."

I chose not to hear this.

"I only want to know if that's your taxi. I'm in a desperate hurry to get somewhere." I did my best to appear accommodating and held my palms up.

"Please," he repeated. "I am talking to God about Jacquine. Her stones are many and painful."

"Then it is your taxi."

He nodded and suddenly I felt foolish for having established the obvious. On the man's shirtsleeve was a large green patch that read "Island Coach Service."

"It's very important," I said. "I need to go to Grande Place."

At this, the man relaxed his formal prayer stance and his narrow eyes perked up with interest.

"You mean to the riot? Where everyone has been arrested?"

I swallowed this down. Everyone, even a praying cab driver in a bare linoleum church, seemed to know more than me.

"Yes, please."

He considered briefly, then nodded as if the matter were as weighty as any of his prayers.

"I can take you there but I need to charge you additional," he said. "Double time for hazard driving. And I can't wait for a return. You'll have to call someone else."

"Fine, fine. But fast."

"I'll let you off a block away and then you can walk. If there are any problems, I'll have to let you out sooner."

"Yes, yes. Can we go?"

Apparently satisfied, the driver then crossed himself twice and rose. Striding quickly, he was suddenly all business and was at the church door and opening it before I could react. The scent of violet water trailed him as he left the room.

"There will be officers all around," he added over his shoulder, as if in justification. "It's no good entering a police action."

He opened the rear door of his taxi and I scrambled in. With the deliberateness of a fussy accountant, he then took a bottle of window cleaner from the front seat and thoroughly wiped down the interior windshield before adjusting the mirrors, putting down the sunshade, and turning on the ignition.

"Please use your safety belt," he said in the rearview mirror as the cab built up speed. "The fine is now 50,000 centimes. I am responsible for your safety." He watched me in the mirror to make sure I complied and then stayed silent for the rest of the drive, which lasted only as long as it took me to comfortably adjust the strap on the belt and open the window.

Turning down a residential block, he abruptly pulled over and took the car out of gear.

"You can walk from here," he said, indicating a deserted street. "Around the next corner and one block more on your left. This is as close as I go." Almost regretfully, he indicated the meter, which showed an exorbitantly high amount of money.

Muttering that the drive didn't seem so hazardous, or long, as to warrant such a price, I nevertheless paid the fare, sans tip, and once again found myself hurrying on foot and breaking out into a new sweat under the afternoon sun.

Still, I was not in so much of a rush that I could not recognize my feelings. That is, I admitted to being extremely nervous. I recalled once being caught on the edges of a riot while covering a longshoremen's strike and it was enough to see the terrified crowd in headlong flight to convince me to immediately put away my notebook and report from safer ground (and never was I so conscious of displaying the press credentials that hung around my neck). I also recall a management enforcer who was guarding the strikebreaking workers but who, when the fighting broke out, went about scattering people with a hammer that he swung violently and in all directions. In at least two occasions I saw, his swings found victims.

So what lay around the corner? (and more to the point, I thought, how does one approach a riot?). Very cautiously, and with the taste of rust having reappeared in my mouth, I girded myself, slowed my step and eased around into the unseen intersection.

And found nothing. In front of me, the entire plaza was like everything I'd encountered so far—eerily at peace. The shops were closed and again there was no human commotion. The only living figure was a skinny older man who sat underneath a store awning midway down the street, smoking and reading a newspaper. I approached him feeling both foolish and apprehensive and thinking that I had somehow misheard Wilkie on the phone. Then I had another startling sensation. As I drew closer, the man looked as if he could be the twin of my recent cab driver. In fact, for one unrestrained moment, I thought it was him and that the driver had simply pulled around the corner, ditched his taxi, and taken up a position on the street. But that this man was wearing different clothes and had a clear, unspotted complexion indicated otherwise.

Before I could come too close, he spoke up.

"Is it Mr. Inoue?" he asked in a braying voice.

By now I was all out of the need to have any explanations. "If there is more to come, let it come," I thought. At least I was expected here.

"Yes. I got here as quickly as I could," I said.

"Mr. Wilkie left a message for you. But first, can I see some identification?"

I reached for my passport and handed it over. The man examined the photo, then gave my identity back.

"My name is Sandros," he said, pulling out a shoebox that lay under his folding chair. "And here is your message." As he opened the box, I saw it was stuffed with hundreds of slips of yellow paper. He plucked one out, gave it to me and went back to his newspaper.

I unfolded the note and saw a half-page of large and perfect script that seemed to have been written by a diligent child's hand. The pertinent lines read, "Mr. MacGower has been arrested and taken to the main government jail. Please come soonest." At the bottom was Wilkie's signature along with the time the message was written, which was approximately a half hour ago. A wave of frustration broke over me. This was not much more information than

I was currently operating with and it seemed profoundly defeating that I should have to work so hard to find out the particulars of such a major event. I crumpled the note and put it in my pocket.

"I'm sorry," I said looking helplessly around at the quiet street, "but wasn't there a riot here?"

"Oh yes, a big one," said Sandros seriously. "One of the candidates was speaking, then another arrived to challenge him, and then the supporters of the two began to fight. Fortunately, the police arrived and used their paint guns to break it up. There were several people arrested and the streets were cleared."

"Paint guns?"

"Yes, it's very effective. No one wants to get their clothes stained or themselves colored. Everyone left immediately."

Now that Sandros mentioned it, I noticed around me that the streets and buildings were streaked with enormous rashes of purple and yellow hues.

"What else happened?" I asked.

Sandros shook his head.

"I came here just as it was ending," he said. "By then, the police trucks were leaving and most of the people were gone." He squinted up at me.

"Is there a message you'd like to leave for Mr. Wilkie?" he asked.

"No message," I said wearily, ready to be hurrying off again to another unknown destination. "But where is the main jail? Is there a taxi stand near here?"

"I doubt if you can find a cab now. All drivers have been ordered off the streets until four p.m."

Sandros indicated a southward direction.

"But the jail is only twenty-two blocks that way and it is a pleasant walk. Not longer than forty minutes. I advise you take the rotunda side so that you might have advantage of the shade. From there, you can also see some of the kapok trees that are in bloom. They offer an impressive sight." He puffed at his cigarette, thinking, then went on.

"Or if you can wait, I will phone my brother. He has a taxi of his own and I'm sure he won't mind taking you for an additional charge. I think he is at church now but I'm sure I can reach him. He is always ready for some extra work."

XXV

IN ITS SMELLS and crumbly institutional facade, the jail was exactly as how I remembered it. Only the people attending it had changed. Now there were officers I did not recognize, as well as a new civilian volunteer, a comely looking young woman whose oversized badge simply read "ERICA." She appeared to be about twenty and to have no duties whatsoever.

Following her, I was led to the same cell that I had occupied a few weeks earlier. But due to the riot, this time the adjoining cages were filled with about a dozen paint-splattered detainees, men and women mixed in together. They looked tired, as if they had been there many hours. Then I recalled my jail experience and one of the first truths that I'd learned from it: that institutionalization is meant to be wearying at every turn.

Owing perhaps to his status, Trevor was being kept in a cell by himself. Bunched around his shoulders was the same dirty down jacket I'd been offered and he clung to it as if he were outdoors on a frigid day. He stood up slowly when I came to the other side of the jail doors.

"You've made it!" he exclaimed.

He extended both of his hands through the bars to grip mine.

"What happened?" I asked.

"A simple thing, as it always is. They needn't concoct complicated reasons to imprison people. When I can be let go?"

I shook my head.

"I don't know. Tell me what happened."

"Later. I must leave at once. The election rests in the balance. I cannot operate from here. Go see what you can do. Now."

Impatiently, he signaled me away, refusing to say anything more, and after a moment of his baleful staring, I left to find someone I could engage on his behalf. Fortunately, though, I only had to go out to the waiting room where I at last discovered Wilkie, who was sitting alone on a wooden bench and eating from a plate of homemade cookies that had just been handed to him by the civilian volunteer.

"Wilkie!" I exclaimed, truly glad to see him. "Tell me what happened."

As I asked him, it also occurred to me that I had been repeating the same question for the last hour without getting much of an answer. My skills as a reporter were obviously in sharp decline, I thought. Thankfully, though, Wilkie was able to provide me a summary of the events and it felt good to finally be able to communicate meaningfully with someone. His story went as such:

Just after I was awakened by Sono's call, Trevor had impulsively decided to stage a last-minute, impromptu campaign rally. "To assess the voters' mood," as he'd put it. Not only did he want to hear what people were talking about, he said, but he also wanted to show gratitude at their support. In reality, though, said Wilkie, Trevor was simply too excited. While resting, he had overheard the reporters on the lawn speculating on his good chances and at that, he could not contain himself indoors.

Setting off with a banner slung across the back of the Renault, he, Wilkie, and the partially clothed Mr. Botolph then began stopping at various polling places so Trevor could mingle with voters and see for himself his own possibilities. At each site, said Wilkie, the noise and the fervor—engineered by Mr. Botolph, who as a concession to events had donned a tight-fitting red sarong—grew until a lengthy, noise-making caravan of supporters became attached to them. Trevor was buoyant, said Wilkie, and for awhile he even sat on the Renault's hood, waving to those on the sidewalk.

For twenty minutes then, their procession meandered ebulliently throughout the city until finally it reached Grande Place, where Trevor had opportunistically spotted a milling throng of people. Unfortunately, though, the crowd had been assembled for a rally in Stanley's honor, and as Trevor's procession drew closer, it became more and more ensnarled by the mob until finally all his cars were forced to a halt. All told, said Wilkie, there were several hundred people at the rally, along with a band, some dignitaries, and television cameras that were airing the event live (had Sono been there too? I wondered). As they arrived, Stanley had just been introduced and was beginning his remarks.

It was this that provoked Trevor into action, said Wilkie. Blocked by the crush around him, yet unable to hold back his feelings at his brother's acclaim, Trevor, infuriated, bolted from the car and pushed his way up to the podium, knocking over a row of elderly Korean War veterans in doing so. Holding aloft the banner he'd torn from the car, he then challenged Stanley to an immediate debate.

At the appearance of Trevor, and then of his followers who'd also left their cars and began shouting for him, the crowd became stunned into momentary confusion. Most began heckling and booing, and wads of paper and other small comets of trash soon started flying toward the stage. Both factions then began chants of support for their respective candidate but since only one of the chants used a first name, it also suddenly appeared as if the entire crowd was shouting for Stanley. Despite this, maintained Wilkie, there was no overt violence. The mood was threatening but things still were peaceable.

But as Trevor continued to argue for his share of the podium, then came the spark that ignited the crowd. Turning to two police officers who were edgily monitoring the situation, Stanley abruptly commanded them to arrest Trevor for instigating a public disturbance. Aghast at the order, the policemen at first pretended not to hear, then began pleading with Stanley to reconsider in view of the circumstances. But Stanley refused to budge, and after receiving more, and more threatening orders, from the vice president, the policemen reluctantly took out their handcuffs and batons.

It was Trevor's being forcibly subdued and shackled that finally pushed the crowd into open conflict, said Wilkie. As he was physically hauled from the podium (the two officers literally dragging him away, all parties entangled in the now-ripped banner), some cheered while others became enraged and a menacing crush developed by the front of the stage. Shoving, punches, and fighting followed, and in an instant one of the nervous policemen fired a warning shot and then the entire crowd was running madly away.

As Wilkie related this, I felt the coldest chill of admiration for Stanley. More than anyone, he'd understood the opportunity that had magically presented itself and made the most of it. Given that several hours still remained for people to vote, arresting the opposing candidate (his brother!) in front of the nation's media was nothing short of a definitive stroke. Indeed, I could not imagine a more life-giving move to Trevor. Surely by now, protests were being organized for him, and at the very least, a rush of voters would be heading for the polls. Yes, I thought grimly, Stanley had recognized and pulled the decisive lever.

Mulling this over, I looked at my watch. The street curfew was scheduled to end in thirty-five minutes.

"Wilkie," I said impulsively, "we have to leave. To make sure that everyone knows that Trevor has been jailed against his rights. That he's been arrested by his brother. We'll hold a press conference at the house. Is your car here?"

"But what about Mr. MacGower?" protested Wilkie. "He's been waiting for you. They haven't filed any charges yet and he's been waiting to be let out."

I looked into Wilkie's broad and uncompromisingly honest face and then did something that pangs me to this day, though it was entirely necessary for I could not have successfully explained my rationale at the moment. I deceived him.

"Don't worry about Trevor," I said as solemnly as I could. "He's safe where he is. He's asked us now to take over. We'd better hurry."

XXVI

MUCH, MUCH LATER—WELL into the small hours of the next day—I found myself stumbling around the dark back garden of Trevor's house with mud on my shoes and a tall sweet drink in my hand. Inside there was still much celebrating (it began at sundown and reached a crescendo when Trevor was released from jail shortly after), and I had joined too strongly in the spirit. I'd begun the night drinking whiskey, then switched to champagne, and now was finishing up with tumblers of rum and cola. Yet it was not from joy that I was indulging but from something else, a curious mix of emotions that I still cannot sum up. In an interview with Sono (for she was still working and needed my words for her story), I tried to summarize this strange boil of feeling but the alcohol interfered and I think I simply babbled to her. At any rate, it was easier to lose oneself in the overall primary emotion of the evening and eventually, that's what I decided to do.

For the day's mandate, though slight, was clear. By a shade of more than one thousand votes, Trevor had been elected president of the Greater Momo-Jiman Republic for the next three years. The results were not yet official but both Van Gland and Stanley had publicly conceded and Trevor had stepped up to claim his victory. Thus by this small margin of individuals a much larger number of people here and worldwide were to be affected, perhaps adversely. That it is a cliché does not detract from its truthfulness: the direction of history often swerves on the pettiest of efforts, and I now included mine in consideration of this particular example.

I was engrossed in this thought and others like it when I turned the corner, tottered along a path of hedgerows and suddenly came face to face with the president-elect. Trevor had one hand against the trunk of a sturdy tree and was preparing to urinate on it.

"The bathroom inside is all full up," he said with some irritation. "I cannot get close to it. In my own house. On the night I am elected president." He grumbled some more, then unzipped himself and unselfconsciously began to wet the ground in front of him.

"There are a lot of supporters here for you," I replied mildly. "Some of them are quite excited." Frankly, I did not want to watch him pee but the soft night air and my own drunkenness served to fix me into place. So instead I looked away from the earth. Upwards towards the sky that tonight showed banks of black-gray clouds and the occasional star. Its night color suddenly reminded me of the small church I had run into earlier that day and the prayers I'd heard for an unknown woman's gall bladder. Already, that seemed like a different existence.

"This is a *fumei* tree," Trevor said gravely, now also staring fixedly into space as he pissed furiously on the tree's roots. He reached out to pat it with his free hand. "A symbol of our native land."

His voice was meant to sound authoritative but I knew no such thing. It was just an old oak, like the dozens that filled my neighborhood in Los Angeles (back home!) and the thousands more I had seen in my life. And as trees went I did not care for it too much. It had an almost willful presence in the face of the many types of climate and terrain in which it was planted; to me, it seemed to place too much of an indiscriminate premium on survival. Nevertheless, concerning its identity I let Trevor have his way.

"In many ways, this tree represents all the hopes and wishes of my people, as well as the dreams I have for them," he continued. "It is a rugged tree, yet beautiful in its way. Its roots are tangled and deep but its limbs stretch high. And though it provides no fruit, the stuff of its core, its bark, is prized in and of itself. We have no national tree so maybe I should make it this one. What do you think?"

"You'll likely have a lot to occupy you at first," I agreed. "Maybe it would be best to concentrate on some smaller matters initially."

"Yes, well," he said, apparently not caring for my characterization of his proposal. He then shook himself out of his reverie, waggled his manhood of its last drops, and put it back in his pants. "Shall we go?"

We began walking back and though I could not tell on which side it was occurring, I noticed that Trevor was limping again. As we strode through the wet grass and came closer to the house, I heard the party noise suddenly break out into a stridulous, higher-pitched realm. Trevor seemed to notice it, too.

"They are celebrating you," I said. "Or at least your victory."

"Then I am in deep trouble," he said with a sudden jot of gloom. "Now I'll have to truly begin watching myself and my actions. I wonder what I'll see."

Remembering our conversation of the night before, I waited for him to say something more but he remained quiet. But because I was curious as to how he might have been affected by that late-night talk, and because we were almost back at the party, I prompted him.

"And what will you have to watch for?"

"The prevailing order of things," he said, instinctively recalling my words to him. "The inborn reversal. When a man achieves his dreams, he becomes marked. An alien figure on the landscape. It's almost as if he's asked, 'What right do you have to realize your desires when most people haven't?'"

"But it's not necessarily dangerous to be singled out so long as you're aware of it," I replied. "Why not enjoy the fruits of your labor? The effort was yours. To appreciate it from the point of completion seems entirely natural."

"Natural but hardly admirable," he said bleakly before stepping back into the clamorous house and disappearing from me for the rest of the evening. "Achieving success is not the most meaningful of outcomes. And having it go to your head is not that eventful of a journey."

XXVII

FOR A FEW days, I turned Trevor's statement over in my mind, trying to see a way into it. It didn't seem to explain him in any way I
had come to know, nor could I trace it to the evolution of anything
that had been gestating inside of him. His was not normally an
inward personality and if he had been working on something of a
philosophical nature, I would have noticed the signs of new mental
development. In the end, I decided to forget about it. Sometimes
the explanation isn't there and sometimes you find that you really
don't want to discover one.

My letting go of this piece of Trevor coincided with my own
trip home. I naturally was glad to get back, even though my return
was clouded by several complications before I left. For one, Rector
Froines refused to pay me my salary. Though he said he felt badly
about it, he maintained that he couldn't condone rewarding me
for a job that ultimately proved in vain. However, I was not too
broken up about this. Truthfully, after seeing the overripe and
deformed fruit he'd sent to the hotel as a gesture of thanks, I'd
expected that he would try to divest himself of his obligations. He
worked with an editor's mind, meaning that he deigned to pay only
on delivery, not effort. Moreover, at the same time, I was grateful
his disappointment didn't manifest itself more harshly toward me
and that in the end, he recognized the circumstances for what they
were (eventually, too, I redeemed myself with him by helping form
a concern that recruited multinationals to Momo-Jima to dig un-

successfully for minerals and thus claim millions in tax write-offs, ventures in which the rector later took his due percentages).

More surprising, and incensing, however, was Stanley's similar refusal to settle with me. Instead, when I went to collect from him, he invited me into his study, then launched into forty minutes of put-upon self-justification to explain his indefensible position (he operated with the writer's view). His main contention was that by arresting Trevor, he alone had triggered the election's outcome. My response that Trevor's success was only made possible by the opportunity I'd engineered went fully unacknowledged (and oddly, it was this lack of acknowledgement, more than the lack of payment, that provoked in me the most anger). In the end, I left the house empty-handed and was tempted to take out my wrath on the Oldsmobile that was again parked on the lawn before I remembered who owned its other half and the time I'd spent in it.

(Fortunately, I haven't seen Stanley since that day. As promised, immediately after the election he packed up his family and resettled somewhere on the Scottish coast, where he secured a cheap secondhand castle and began his bid for royalty. Since then, however, I've read that his part of the northern countryside has been inundated by the worst winter in decades, with roads and basic services washed out, mud walls as high as ten feet, and the town of Grimspew all but obliterated under a cataclysm of frozen earth. For someone who staked his life on the caprices of geography, such calamities must be overwhelming, I've since thought with pleasure.)

As for Trevor, I do see him regularly and that is because in return for my services, he has appointed me Momo-Jiman consul to the US, based in Los Angeles (Trevor was also the only one who paid me my salary, paltry as it was). For this I fly monthly to Momo-Jima and brief him on matters ranging from American politics to developments in global economics to the reviews of the latest movies, including video releases. I also counsel him concerning his performance in office, though this mostly entails listening to his lengthy and self-obsessed monodramas, which, since he has been elected, he has had fewer chances to deliver. But as this assignment allows me to see Sono (while flying for free on Guanche Air and keeping Wilkie as my assistant) and only requires that I spend a few weekly hours clipping articles and keeping conversant with world affairs, I am glad for it.

But where this leaves me overall, I am not sure. While I've never thought it was in my best interests to depend too much on my feelings for my future, I find myself startled by the strength of some of my emotions and the directions they point me in, particularly in regards to Sono and her view of things. Perhaps I am thinking it is time to settle into a semi-permanent sort of rhythm, one that might generate a significant mosaic of people and history. These are, I tell myself, an entirely natural set of thoughts to be having at my age. Yet, alone in my apartment in Los Angeles, I feel her absence palpably and at times, intolerably.

(Sono, of course, opposes this. She is of the belief that I am fully incapable of lending myself to any sort of permanency and that for me to believe I can is a delusion of which she will have no part. But, as she adds, she is of the same inconstant nature and therein lies her attraction to me. It is an unresolvable, but not unappealing situation.)

But back to my burgeoning feelings of attachment. I find I get them most strongly as I'm returning to Momo-Jima and the airplane begins its slow spiral descent over the still South Pacific waters. From above, I am always startled by how strikingly beautiful the island is, embedded like a brown anthracite in surrounding deep sapphire. From above, I feel very much in kinship with it, similar to a protective parent watching over an undersized child. Sitting in the cabin, my state then becomes reflective, yet oddly upbeat. My emotions culminate when the flight attendant takes the intercom to cheerfully announce, "Welcome, you have arrived in Momo-Jima."

It is then, for a brief and incandescent moment, that I can almost believe I have.

Biographical Note

Scott Shibuya Brown is a former staff correspondent for *Time Magazine* and a staff writer for the *Los Angeles Times*. He lives in Los Angeles, where he teaches at California State University, Northridge, and plays in the punk band Finland Station.